A FAMILY AFFAIR: THE CHOICE

MARY CAMPISI

MARY CAMPISI BOOKS, LLC

INTRODUCTION

If Ben Reed could have guessed at the event that would hurl him into danger and set off a chain reaction that threatened his marriage, his family, his health, *and* his future in Magdalena, he would not have said it would occur at home. For a man who'd served his country, chased bad guys, and thrust himself into the middle of danger more often than not, his house was his safe haven, not a battle zone.

And maybe that's why Ben never saw the accident coming.

As a physical therapist, Gina knows the toll a long rehabilitation can take on a person, *and* a relationship. Her husband's perpetual moodiness, sullen attitude, and refusal to continue therapy create a battleground that's about to explode. In desperation, Gina turns to the new physical therapist in town who's been dubbed the Angel of Hope and Healing.

For a busted-up and beaten-down guy who questions his worth and ability to be what he once was, the beautiful physical therapist is just the balm he needs to assure him he can have *anything* he wants. By the time Ben realizes the woman's interested in more than his recovery, a scandal erupts that makes Gina believe he's betrayed her.

Now, Ben must win back his wife's trust or risk the greatest heartache of all—a life without her. Of course, he's going to need help, and isn't offering guidance and help Magdalena's specialty?

P.S. Did you know Harry's going to rescue a dog? Oh, you won't want to miss this one! I like to think of it as *The rescued rescues a rescue.*

Truth in Lies Series
Book One: *A Family Affair*
Book Two: *A Family Affair: Spring*
Book Three: *A Family Affair: Summer*
Book Four: *A Family Affair: Fall*
Book Five: *A Family Affair: Christmas*
Book Six: *A Family Affair: Winter*
Book Seven: *A Family Affair: The Promise*
Book Eight: *A Family Affair: The Secret*
Book Nine: *A Family Affair: The Wish*
Book Ten: *A Family Affair: The Gift*
Book Eleven: *A Family Affair: The Weddings*, a novella
Book Twelve: *A Family Affair: The Cabin*, a novella
Book Thirteen: *A Family Affair: The Return*
Book Fourteen: *A Family Affair: The Choice*
Book Fifteen: *A Family Affair: The Proposal*
A Family Affair Boxed Set: Books 1-3
A Family Affair Boxed Set 2: Books 4-6
Meals From Magdalena: A Family Affair Cookbook

eBook ISBN: 978-1-942158-43-1

Print ISBN: 978-1-942158-45-5

❀ Created with Vellum

DEDICATION

An animal's love is pure, simple, absolute. R.I.P. Cooper Campisi, beloved rescue dog, most loyal friend, and companion (2007-2018)

This book is dedicated to my readers whose four-legged family members crossed the Rainbow Bridge. We are part of a "pack" and our animals will live in our hearts forever. Thank you for the emails, the stories, and pictures of your most beloved furry friends. I am truly touched. I've listed 216 names, in alphabetical order, of pets who have crossed the Rainbow Bridge, and even a few who are still with us. Again, many thanks for sharing. I know Cooper is chasing tennis balls and making new friends.

Abbey Jackson, Amber, Amber, Amy, Angel, Augie, Avalon, Baby, Barney, Barrable Jabble, Beasley, Beauty, Bella, Belle, Benjamin, Benji, Bessie, Bitsy, Blue, Bo(Hobo), Bourbon, Bruno, Bubba, Buck, Buddy, Buddy, Bueller, Buffy, Buffy, Buster, Buster Brown, Buster Dee, Carrie, Charis, Charlie, Charlie, Chase, Cheeka, Chester, Chloe, Chow-Lin, Cody, Compani Getty, Cooper, Cosmo, Creed, Crispin,

Crystal, Cuddles, Daisy, Deacon, Derry, Diamond, Diamond, Diamond, Dixie, Druscilla, Ellie, Elsie, Elvis, Emma, Emma, Emma Jean Harris, Emmie, Esme Angel, Ezra, Fifi, Filbie, Frankie, Gazoo, Geisha, George, Ginnie Jackson, Gizmo, Goober, Guiness, Gusto, Harriet, Havyn, Heidi, Heidi, Hello Kitty, Honey Szmytke, Jack Russell, Jake, Jake, Jasmine, Jazz, Jelli Bean, Jofa, JoJo, Jumpy, Junior, Katie, Keech, Keeper, Keisha, Kel, Kelly, Kim, Kitty Henry Brennar, Koa, LaBelle Patrick, Linus, Little One, Louie J, Lucy, Lucy, Luke, Luther, Mad Max, Max, Max, Maxwell, McTavish, Merlin, Michigan, Miriah, Missa, Missy, Molly, Molly, Molly(Milly Molly Mandy Moo Cow), Morning Star, Mr. Austen Darcy, Muffin, Murphy, Nala, Neesha, Nilla, Oliver, Onyx, Oreo, Osa, Ozzie, Pat, Patches, Patches Norman, Peaches, Peanut, Pedro, Penny, Pepper, Percy, Petey, PJ, Pogo, Polly, Powder, Princess, Puella, Ralphie, Rex, Rocko, Rocky, Ruth Ann, Sadie, Sam, Sam, Sammie Sambone, Samonoska, Sampson, Sandy, Sandy, Sasha, Shadow, Shadow, Shayla Corbin, Sheba, Sheba, Shiva, Skeeter, Smokey, Snickers, Snoopy, Snoopy, Snow, Snowflake, Spaz, Spookie Man, Spot, Spot, Stinker, Stonewall, Sue, Sugar, Sunshine, Tabitha, Teddy, Tenner, Teresa, Thunder, Toby, Toby, Tom, Tori, Tucker, Tugger, Tugger Bear, Western Star, Willow, Woody, Wyatt, Zak, Zane, Zoe, Zoey, Zoey

And our furry friends who have not crossed the Rainbow Bridge: Abbeygale, Gunnar, JayJay, Lacy, Maggie, Roscoe D'Angelo, Trooper

1

If Ben Reed could have guessed at the event that would hurl him into danger and set off a chain reaction that threatened his marriage, his family, his health, and his future in Magdalena, he would not have said it would occur at home. For a man who'd served his country, chased bad guys, and thrust himself into the middle of danger more often than not, his house was his safe haven, not a battle zone.

And maybe that's why Ben never saw the accident coming. He'd relaxed, gone soft, and forgotten the world could be cruel and life would nail you the second you stopped paying attention. The event that damaged his body and his universe did not come from a police-related incident. No stray bullets, no car chases, no thugs. Those threats belonged to a past where threats and risky situations were acknowledged, at times even embraced as a way to fuel the adrenaline rush and snuff out gaps in a lonely existence. But here, in Magdalena, Ben Reed had become a transformed man: loving husband, devoted father, good friend, responsible citizen. He even delivered food to the needy, drove a few pets *and* their owners to the vet, and joined in the annual Magdalena run to good health.

Gina still worried when he wore his police uniform, mostly because she overanalyzed the potential threats versus the non-threats of police work in Magdalena, where loud music, misplaced keys, and an expired parking meter were the usual. But twelve days before Christmas, the woman he'd slept beside every night, mother of his two children, and heart of his soul, had not anticipated the threat attached to her latest request, one that involved a ladder and a life-sized plastic snowman.

His wife had been after him to get the rest of the Christmas boxes from the attic and set up the snowman on the front porch, but why did she have to send him those damn reminders? In the form of a list? Updated on a weekly, often twenty-four-hour basis? He knew it was Gina's way of dealing with control issues stemming from that screwed-up family of hers, and most of the time he went along with it. But some days he ignored the requests, not because he didn't plan to complete the list or because he didn't love his wife. Some days, it was more about assessing and prioritizing, an area he and Gina didn't always agree on. Gina flagged everything as a level-one priority, even if it were as insignificant as picking up an extra loaf of bread when there were already two in the freezer. Ben considered that third loaf of bread an off-the-radar non-necessity, right along with vitamins and wearing sunscreen.

He'd planned to climb into the attic tomorrow afternoon and drag down the snowman and the rest of the boxes they'd accumulated in their four years together. Today was football-beer-chili day at Cash's. Nate would be there, too, and they planned to discuss the upcoming Christmas gift deliveries to the families in need. Okay, so there'd be more eating, drinking, and football game watching, but they'd figure out the Christmas delivery schedule at some point. Hadn't Nate said Christine created a spreadsheet with names and addresses compiled by The Bleeding Hearts Society?

The delivery schedule had doubled since last year, thanks to the anonymous donation they'd received. Yeah, right. Anonymous, as in Harry Blacksworth. The guy was too damn humble, but he was straight-out serious about not attaching his name to the goodwill efforts in town. There'd been The Bleeding Hearts Society's "Seeds for Sadie" event, the firemen's "Flames and Franks," and the local rescue's "Pounds for Pets" weightlifting competition. When people asked if Harry had a part in them, he'd shrug and toss out the standard *No idea what you're talking about.* If they persisted, he'd laugh and say, *Do I look like a do-gooder to you?* The guy was a softie with a heart as big as his bank account and the town was lucky to count him as one of their own.

What man would ignore a big game to host a get-together for a bunch of women and their kids? Harry Blacksworth, no question there. Harry and Greta had invited Gina, Christine, Tess, and the kids to their house for a Christmas lunch and craft session. Of course, Lily Desantro had most likely orchestrated the event, but Harry was in the middle of it with his big laugh, fancy clothes, and wide smiles. No doubt he and Lily had created an "event" to remember, one Gina might recommend Ben, Nate, and Cash participate in should the opportunity arise again as in *Life is not all about silly ball games.*

Weeks and months later, Ben would wish he'd decided against the chili-beer-football day and joined his wife and kids for whatever pre-Christmas event the man in the mansion had going on. That choice would have prevented a world of heartache. Minutes before the disaster that changed his life, Ben helped buckle the kids into their car seats, leaned through the car window, and kissed his wife. "Have a good time. Bring a Christmas cookie or two home for me."

"Greta's already got a few packed away, just for you."

Gina rarely ate sweets and despite her careful calorie counting, exercise, and strong will, those post-baby pounds hung around. That bothered her. A lot. Ben thought she looked perfect, but when a woman gets it in her head she's carrying extra pounds that make her less attractive, all a man can do is prove her wrong—which Ben did, in and out of bed.

"Thank you for getting the boxes in the attic."

He still got lost in those dark eyes when she looked at him like that. "You're welcome."

Her voice shifted, dipped. "And Mr. Snowman."

How could a guy say no to that voice? "And Mr. Snowman." Ben smiled, stroked her cheek. "Have a good time. I'll see you later."

Those dark eyes sparkled. "Thank you."

"You can thank me later." The blush said she knew exactly what he meant.

After, he would say it was that damn smile and the opportunity to make his wife happy that caused the accident. And when anger swirled in his gut and spread through him, he'd blame his wife's incessant list-making and desire to control life as the culprit behind the accident. But in the quiet moments of the night, he would have to admit that he'd just been in too damn much of a hurry and *that* had been his undoing.

Ben waited until Gina and the kids headed down the street before he rushed to the detached garage, opened the door, and stepped inside. How many boxes were still in the attic? Three? Six? He checked his watch, calculated the time it would take to shower and get to Cash's before game time. If he hurried, he could have everything sitting in the living room, ready to go for tomorrow's decorating. Their son, Alex, had been hounding him to get the darn Snowman down for three days. *Dad, why is Mr. Snowman still in the attic? Dad, Mr. Snowman is going to miss Christmas if you don't get him down.*

Ben grabbed the stepladder, opened it, and climbed up the rungs. He should have replaced the creaky thing this summer, but why spend the money when he only used it a few times a year? Still, he guessed he should check into one of those fiberglass stepladders for next year. He pulled open the hatch to the attic, heaved himself into the opening, and found the pull-chain light. There were still five boxes and the life-size Mr. Snowman. How had they accumulated so much Christmas stuff in four short years? He knew the answer to that one, didn't even have to think about it. He and Gina wanted to create holiday memories filled with joy and happiness, the kind neither of them had growing up. They would be the parents they wished they'd had...

Ben lifted two cardboard boxes marked with Gina's fancy label maker, listing the items in the box. He scrambled down the ladder maneuvering one box and then the next to the floor. When he dumped the fifth box on top of the others, he blew out a sigh and headed up the ladder after Mr. Snowman. Ben dragged the big guy to the opening of the attic, wished the guy's belly were a bit slimmer or the attic opening a bit wider. He stood on the sixth rung of the ladder, eased the plastic snowman through the opening, nice and slow. Then the darn thing stuck, right at the belly. Ben gave it a few gentle tugs that inched it forward...one big pull should do it. That *big pull* proved his undoing. As his foot slipped, he grabbed the rungs, but his strength toppled the ladder and landed him on the cement floor, knee first. Pain. White hot. Bone-deep. Ben lay on the cement floor for several minutes eyeballing the light sifting through the attic opening. He sucked in air, fought through the pain as he worked his cell phone from his jeans pocket, and dialed 9-1-1.

GINA GOT the call as they were sprinkling glitter on poinsettia petals. Lily loved glitter, called it *sparkly*, and made her think of stars, which made her think of heaven. When Gina's cell phone rang, she figured it was Ben with a question about the boxes or Mr. Snowman. Her husband knew of her obsession with organization and details and had half joked that one day he'd steal every notepad and pen in the house. He said he'd take her phone, too, so she couldn't text him lists either. Of course, he'd never do it, and she had been trying to relax the list making, but with a husband, a job, two children, and a house to run, a person needed a list or two, didn't she?

But this call wasn't from Ben. When Gina answered, a woman's voice filled the line: professional, concerned. "Gina?"

"Yes?"

"This is Helen Donaldson from the ER. How are you?"

Gina answered with a hesitant, "Fine." Why was Helen calling her? They'd had coffee and talked about their kids a few times, but she wouldn't say they were friends.

"It's Ben. There's been an accident. Can you get here as soon as possible?"

Ben? A mix of shock and dread slid through Gina, landed in her brain. "Accident?" She clutched the phone, sipped air. She should have reminded him how slippery the back roads to Cash's could get when it snowed. Ben was a city boy; what did he know about winding roads and curves with flimsy guardrails? The SUV he drove was not a performance vehicle like the ones he used to drive. Gina sipped more air, her brain compiling scenarios contributing to the accident. She bet the darn tires were behind it all. Why had she listened to him when he told her the tread would last until spring? Why hadn't she forced him to get new ones? *Why had she not trusted her gut?*

"Gina?" Helen's voice pulled her back. "Can you have someone drive you to the hospital?"

"I can drive myself. I just have to get someone to watch the—"

"Gina, give me the phone." Harry Blacksworth stood before her, hand outstretched, tanned face a mix of concern and determination. When she offered him the phone, he squeezed her shoulder, nodded, and headed into the other room, head bent, voice low as he spoke to Helen.

For someone who'd spent most of her life trying to manage and anticipate outcomes, Gina knew deep down there was only so much a person could do. The rest was up to fate, or what others referred to as destiny. Some might pin a situation on bad luck or good fortune, depending on the person and the event. Ben didn't talk about fate, destiny, good or bad luck; he talked about protection. That's what he believed in, and he'd vowed to be her protector. *You're my heart, Gina. I'll always protect you. I won't let anything happen to you.* What she'd wanted to say so many times and couldn't, smothered her heart, filled her with grief. *I'll protect you, Ben. You're my heart, my soul. I can't let anything happen to you.*

But she had.

She didn't realize she was crying until Christine handed her a tissue and said in a soft voice, "Uncle Harry will drive you to the hospital and we'll take care of the kids. You go and be with Ben."

Tess laid a hand on her arm, her voice cracking when she spoke. "We're here for you."

They'd all known their share of tragedies and helped each other through them. Nate and Christine had been driven apart by her mother's desire for vengeance. Tess and Cash had suffered a breakup, the loss of a child Cash didn't know about, the pain of infertility, and so much more. Bree wasn't here, but she'd known the loss of a child and the pain of her husband's infidelity. Was it Gina's turn? She could *not* lose Ben. Their children needed him. *She* needed him. She would not lose the only man she'd ever truly loved. Gina blotted her tears, cleared her throat, and turned to Harry. "I'm ready."

When Gina entered Magdalena General Hospital a short while later with Harry Blacksworth's firm grasp on her arm, she took in her surroundings. How many times had she walked these halls as a physical therapist, determined to help patients with therapy sessions and encouragement that would get them back to a healthy lifestyle, or as close to it as possible? *Time, patience, and attitude* she'd say as she guided them through the routines. In some cases, it was about acceptance, but Gina never gave up on the patient or the power of believing in one's capabilities. She glanced toward the sign for the maternity ward, thought of her children's births. Alex's had been unpredictable and scary, but Ben had been there for her, right up until he passed out, an occurrence he'd sworn had to do with low blood sugar. They'd all let him think they believed him, but the truth was, fear had taken her husband down, faster than a double jab to the gut. Gina felt that fear now, thought she might pass out or throw up...

Harry steadied her when she stumbled. "Hang on, Gina. We're almost there."

It took a man of courage to walk into the same emergency room where he almost lost his wife a few years before. Everyone had heard of Greta Blacksworth's fall that landed her in the new pool she and Harry had built. Word had it Harry dove in, fancy clothes and all, and pulled her out of the water, but it had been her son AJ who called 9-1-1 and calmed Harry until the EMTs arrived.

Gina glanced at Harry, noted the paleness about the lips, the too-bright eyes. He was thinking about Greta and how he almost lost her. "Harry, you don't have to stay here. I'll be fine."

"To hell with that," he said in a gruff voice. "I'm not leaving until we have answers. Nate and Cash should be here soon, so hang on, okay?"

She nodded, her brain numb. "Okay. Harry?" Gina didn't want to ask this next question, but she had to know because the not knowing was so much worse. "Where did the accident happen? It was on the road to Cash's, wasn't it?" He stared at her as if he didn't understand the question. What was he hiding? "Harry, just tell me, please."

The man people called big-hearted and soft placed his hands on her shoulders, said in a gentle voice, "This wasn't a car accident, Gina. He fell off the ladder in the garage."

FRACTURED TIBIAL PLATEAU. Left sided bruising. Laceration to the chin and cheek. Harry said the EMTs found Ben on the garage floor with the ladder on top of him. *Good thing he had his phone with him and managed to call 9-1-1*, Harry had said. *Your husband knows how to keep his head, even when he's busting with pain.* Of course, Harry must be thinking of his own 9-1-1 emergency situation, where he'd panicked. Ben didn't panic; military and police training had taught him to stay calm, assess, and react.

Gina had once believed she possessed the same ability to remain calm, assess, and react, but that changed the day Ben Reed walked into Magdalena and her life. That's when she opened up and started to feel again, to risk love and hurt, and that's when she realized she was not calm or objective where her husband or his safety was concerned. Same with their two children. How could she keep them safe from the hazards found in everyday living that could snuff out a young life in seconds? Meningitis, falls, poisons. It didn't matter that most of this was unreasonable because Gina Reed wanted to assure their health, safety, and darn it, their happiness. But she'd known all along that she couldn't; life and destiny would take over and no matter how much she tried, she could not protect them from either.

Gina sat in the vinyl chair next to her husband's bed, her hand resting on his arm as he slept. She touched his skin, checked his pulse, studied the rise and fall of his chest. Yes, there were monitors beeping next to him, two IV bags, and a pain-relief button, all part of his post-surgical care, but she needed to provide her own monitoring—to be a part of him. She blew out a quiet sigh, settled her gaze on his face, still so handsome despite the pallor beneath the tan, the bruised area covering the gash on his chin and cheek. *Oh, Ben, I am so sorry you have to go through this.* She sniffed, swiped at her cheeks. *So very sorry. I wish I'd never asked you to get those darn decorations from the attic.* Tiny shreds of guilt clung to her, refused to go away. Why hadn't she just let him go to Cash's and watch the ballgame? They'd be home now, snuggled in bed next to each other, his arm flung around her middle, his breath deep, even. Why had she insisted he finish his jobs before he took off? She should not have coaxed Alex to tell his father *Mr. Snowman is going to miss Christmas if you don't get him down.*

"Hey, Gina."

She glanced at the doorway, spotted Cash Casherdon moving toward her with a cloth bag stamped *Dog Lover.* "Hi, Cash. I'm sorry you had to make another trip, and I wouldn't have asked you if—"

"No worries." He set the bag on the table. "I wanted to see the old boy for myself." His gaze slid to his former partner, and Gina didn't miss the pain that flashed across his face seconds before he buried it. "He's a tough pain-in-the butt; he'll be okay."

"Thanks." Cash didn't know that any more than he knew what a fractured tibial plateau really meant, but she appreciated the words. He and Nate had been there throughout the surgery and didn't head home until Ben was in recovery. Harry Blacksworth stayed, too, patted her hand, whispered to her about hanging tough and trusting the doctors to do what they did best. Nate didn't say much, but the expression on his face said he understood what she was going through: the angst, the worry, the fear...maybe even the guilt.

"So—" he pulled out two Pink Lady apples and an Asian

salad mix "—we've got apples and salad. Tess said they're your favorites." He rifled around in the bag, removed a tooth-brush, toothpaste, a small baggie of chicken, and a packet of salad dressing. "More stuff."

She'd asked him to have Tess pack an overnight bag for her and gather up things for the kids because she had no idea how long she'd be at the hospital. Tess would do what needed done, and so would Christine, Bree, and their husbands. They would stick together and help Ben, Gina, and the kids find their way back to normal. It would take patience, faith, and a commitment from Ben therapy-wise, no matter how aggravating or slow the process or the results. That would be the tricky part because Ben was not used to a body that failed him or a recovery timetable that extended for several months.

But he would have to get used to it. They all would. Because this was their new normal.

"WHAT DO you mean I can't put weight on my left leg?" Ben squinted at his wife through a haze of drugs and pain. "How am I supposed to walk?" He slid a glance at the brace on his left leg, squinted again.

"You'll use crutches." Gina squeezed his arm, said in a gentle voice, "The kind of fracture you have is pretty serious, Ben. It's called a tibial plateau fracture."

He swung his gaze to hers, frowned. "Can you say that in English?"

"You broke the top of your shin bone below the knee."

"So?" He rubbed his jaw, blew out a harsh breath. "Lots of people mess up their knees, and they bounce right back after a little therapy." What was a broken bone or a busted knee to a guy like him? "It's not like I'm some couch potato. I'm an athlete, Gina; my body isn't going to fail me, and a busted knee won't stop me." Did she not know the endurance he had, the muscle strength and determination? "How long do I have to use crutches?" He figured a week, maybe two...

"It's a slow process..."

That wasn't an answer. "A slow process for what? To not use crutches?" He tried to understand, but the pain meds blurred the meaning behind her words.

"A slow process to recover—" she paused, licked her lips "—from the injury."

"How slow?" What were they talking about here?

"It could take months."

"Months?" The word gut-punched him. *Months?* That was one thing about his wife, she didn't believe in sugar coating the truth. Not Gina. She subscribed to straight-up answers and to hell with a guy's need to understand it a piece at a time. "Months," he repeated, stretching out the word. "Two? Three? Four? Ten?" When she didn't answer, he clutched her hand. "Gina? Just tell me, damn it."

Those dark eyes grew bright. "Every patient is different, so it's hard to say."

Right. Even in his drug-induced state, he could tell she didn't want to answer. "But what about *this* patient, your husband? How long could it take *me* to recover?"

She shrugged. "The tibial plateau is a crucial part of the weight-bearing process," she said as though reciting to a class of physical therapy students and not her husband. "It carries load and is responsible for knee alignment, stability, and motion. You fractured it when you fell off the ladder. You were fortunate there weren't any anterior cruciate ligament or meniscus ligament tears."

Fortunate, yeah, that's what he'd call it. "And now what?"

Gina continued with what he should have seen coming if he were on full alert: the plan according to his ever-organized, by-the-book wife. "The doctor will want to start physical therapy pretty much right away. Nothing strenuous, but we have to make sure you don't get tight. There's a passive motion machine, seated leg lifts, low resistance bands..."

Ben tried to shift his weight to get more comfortable, winced. "Wow. Big stuff."

"It *is* big stuff, Ben. It's important stuff."

The tone and the frown said she didn't like his comments. "What should I do, jump up and down and shout my excitement that I'll be allowed to lift my leg?" It was his turn to frown. "Oh, right. I can't jump up and down because I can't bear weight, can I?" The frown shifted to a scowl. "Just give me a time frame, a loose one will do." When she hesitated, he pushed on. "I won't hold you to it but give me something."

"As long as you understand this is just a reference and not specific to you."

He nodded. "Sure, references, not specific to me."

"I've only dealt with a few cases and none of them were as fit as you, but my best guess is no weight bearing for six weeks or so. Then you'll start at twenty-five percent. Therapy will include exercises for stretching, strengthening, and stability—"

"How long until I'm back to normal?" When she hesitated, he pressed on, "Just a guess."

"A guess?" She squeezed his hand, held his gaze, and poured out the truth that busted his world apart. "Maybe six months."

"Six months?" That was half a year of his life...two seasons...an eternity...

Gina's next words covered him, stuffed with hope and a plan. "The hardest part of this whole process will be patience. You're a doer and a fixer, and it's going to be very difficult to let others, especially me, help you." Her voice cracked. "But you have to let me help you, Ben." She lifted his hand to her lips, kissed each knuckle. "We'll get through this together, you'll see. Everything will be all right."

2

———

Harry would never forget the day his best friend walked into his life. He was on his way back from Renova thinking about the bowl of penne and spinach with garbanzo beans Greta had waiting for him. It had snowed again last night, making it six straight days of the white stuff. Harry didn't mind snow, neither did the kids, who begged him to help build a fort, make a snowman, go sledding...

Who would have thought Harry Blacksworth could hold down a fort and make a snowball better than Nate Desantro? Hell, who would have thought Harry could do *anything* better than anyone else besides hold his liquor? But if Lily thought Harry's snowballs were the *perfect size and the perfect roundness*, even better than her brother's, who was he to argue?

Thinking of Lily and snow made him remember those blasted snow angels she loved so much, the ones she said were best created at night, under the stars, so you could talk to people in heaven. Like her dad. Harry choked up every damn time he thought about it, but Lily was right. The snow-angel-looking-up-at-the-stars gig was a great way to talk to Charlie.

Kids. What had he ever done without them? And Lily? How had she walked this earth for fourteen years before he found her? Well...he knew the answer to that one and it wasn't a good or happy one, but sometimes adult screw-ups led to miracles. And Lily Desantro sure was a miracle. So was Greta, and AJ, Lizzie, and Jackson.

Harry rounded a bend and hit a straight stretch of road. *What the hell...?* He squinted against the glare of sun and snow, spotted an animal several yards away. Black, long, lean, lit up by the sun as he trotted toward Harry, the guy could be anywhere between fifty to eighty pounds. Harry slowed the SUV, waited as the animal picked up speed. Were those ears flapping? And was that a patch of white on its chest? Was that a *dog*? Damn, it *was* a dog! Harry pulled off the road, considered the intelligence of approaching a dog in the wild who could have rabies or who knew what. He should call animal control and file a report. They'd know what to do. Or maybe he should call Ben Reed. Nope, couldn't call Ben because he was on leave due to the accident. He could call him anyway; the guy probably wouldn't mind. Harry stared at the dog who'd made his way to the passenger side of the SUV and stared right back at him, mouth open, tail wagging.

He could call Nate and see what he knew about dogs in the wild. Strays, that's what they were called, weren't they? But Nate would ask too many questions and he could imagine the snide comments that would continue weeks and months later. The guy already had enough ammunition to use against Harry without giving him more. Nate was out. Ben was out. Greta? Nope, not Greta. He considered AJ for a half second, but the boy was in school and it might not be a good idea to call him to the main office for a phone call about how to handle a stray dog.

Harry sucked in a breath, muttered *What the hell*, and opened the door. "Here, dog." He eased his way to the passenger side, loafers crunching in the snow, and eyed the dog. The mutt ran toward him, jumped up, his diamond-shaped white chest level with Harry's waist, paws swiping at Harry's cashmere coat. "Hey, hey. Down. Down!" The dog left a muddy paw-print trail on the tan cashmere, nuzzled his nose against Harry's crotch, and wagged his tail so hard his whole body wriggled. "Okay, okay." Harry patted the dog's head, searched for a collar. None. No surprise there. "Where'd you come from—" he leaned down, checked the animal's private area "—boy? Huh, where'd you come from?"

Big brown soulful eyes met his, pulled him in, stole his heart. What were the odds that a stray dog would happen along a country road that Harry hadn't traveled in two months? No identification, no sign of a home for miles...almost as if he'd been plopped in front of Harry with no past. But everybody had a past, even dogs, and if the scrawny body and visible ribcage were any indication, this guy's hadn't been good. That was all about to change, because Harry could rescue him, give him hope and a second chance, just like Greta had done for him. Maybe he should have thought things through before he decided to keep the dog, or at least talked to Greta about it, but he didn't. Nope, that wasn't Harry's style; he was more of a jump-in-first-and-call-for-help-later kind of guy. "How about you come home with me, huh? You can have your own bed. Hell, you can have your own room if you want." The dog wagged his tail, barked. Harry laughed and rubbed a hand along the dog's back. "Yup, you like the sound of that, don't you, boy?"

An hour, two bathroom messes, and a puke later, Harry realized he probably *should* have consulted with Greta before strolling into the house with a dog. Once the kids spotted the guy, they were all over him, throwing Jackson's ball, running around the house, trying out names. Greta eyed Harry with that how-could-you-have-been-so-foolish look that let him know the baby had more common sense than he did.

Harry eyed the dog who sprawled on the kitchen floor three feet away, eyeing him back. "I'm sorry, Greta, guess I screwed up, huh?"

His wife's lips pinched, and she said in that no-nonsense tone she used with the kids when they forgot to flush the toilet, "A dog is a big responsibility, Harry, not just a plaything to put in a corner when you're done."

That sounded a lot like the relationships he'd had in his former life, before Greta. *Play time and then see you later.* "I know, I know, but I couldn't leave him on that road all by himself." He pointed to the dog's ribs. "Bet he's been on his own for a while. You've got to miss more than a few meals to have ribs like that. And what are those marks behind his ears, did you see those?" Harry stood, moved toward the dog, and leaned down to inspect an ear.

"Life is full of sad stories, Harry, including this dog's, but unless you are willing to make a one-hundred percent commitment, you shouldn't keep him."

Shouldn't keep him? His gut spurted up bits of the penne and spinach he'd eaten for lunch. What was it about this guy that made him desperate to give him a better life? A second chance? He'd never been an animal person, had never even owned a fish, but those eyes and that face? Harry patted the dog's head, smiled when the metronome tail-wagging started, and said in a gruff voice, "I'll do it, Greta. I don't want this guy to ever go hungry again, or not have a place to sleep...or be alone...or afraid..."

"And you are willing to do what needs done?" That German accent drilled him in rapid staccato before he could answer. "Walk him, feed him, clean up his messes, take him to the vet? You will do all of that? And you will not complain or try to pay AJ or Lizzie to do it for you?"

Greta made having a dog sound like a punishment. Sure, it was work, but what about the rewards? Didn't dogs improve people's moods? Calm them and provide company? Make a person happier? "I'll do it all and I won't bribe the kids to help." Though he had thought AJ could make a few extra bucks doing poop patrol...

"Of course, they would have to help because that will teach them *responsibility*."

She enunciated that last word like he might not understand it. He knew what it meant, knew all about it, even if he chose to ignore it at times. "Sure, they should learn responsibility."

Greta slid a notepad and pen toward him. "You'll need to make a list of what he'll need, starting with a vet appointment."

Harry slid his wife a smile, grabbed the pad and pen. "Don't you think we should start with a name?"

She let out a sigh. "Do you have one in mind?"

The smile spread. "Cooper."

"Cooper?"

"It's perfect." Harry knelt on the floor, rubbed the dog's belly. "Did you ever see *High Noon* with Gary Cooper?" When his wife shook her head, he shrugged and continued, "It's an old film about a former marshal who's planning to leave town with his bride when news that an outlaw he once turned in is coming after him. You know, the classic revenge-type stuff. The whole town turns coward on him and he's got to face the outlaw alone. I won't say more in case you want to watch it, but when I spotted this guy, the sun was big and bright, and we were the only ones on the road. It made me think of Gary Cooper in that movie."

"Cooper," she repeated, studying the dog.

"Cooper Blacksworth." Harry laughed. "Welcome to the family."

Eight days later, Harry knew why people didn't get dogs. They came into your life, stole your heart, and made it three times bigger than it was. You engaged in silly antics like singing to them, talking *for* them, hell, constantly talking *about* them. And just when you couldn't imagine life without them, they broke your heart by dying and there wasn't a damn thing you could do about it.

Like now. Cooper hadn't gulped his last breath, but it was coming, just like the next snowfall. Maybe it would have been better to let him run the roads instead of forcing house rules and civilization on him. Who was he kidding? The dog didn't seem to mind a fenced-in yard or a bunch of windows separating him from the chipmunks, squirrels, and birds he eyeballed like they were treats. It was Harry and his pain-in-the-ass heart that was the problem. He'd fallen for the damn dog and now he might lose him.

"Harry?" Greta laid a hand on his arm, her voice soft and gentle, the way she spoke to the kids when a thunderstorm scared them. "We need to talk about this."

He did not want to talk about it, not when the outcome was bleak and his heart was splitting right down the middle.

But his wife wasn't going to let it go, so he might as well spit out the pain and be done with it. "I know what you're think-ing. He's just a dog. You can get another one, no big deal." The words made Harry queasy, but he pushed on, fear and anger spilling from his mouth. "He is *not* just a dog, Greta. Can't you see that?" His voice wobbled, split open with pain. "The damn mutt reminds me too much of myself and no matter what it takes, we've got to help him because I can't lose him."

"Harry, take a breath."

There was that voice again, soothing, kind. He slid Greta a look, muttered, "What?" Her next words would be a mix of reason and patience and he did not want to hear them. Damn it, all he wanted was an assurance that Cooper would be around next Christmas so he could use the stocking Lizzie bought him two days ago. Was that too much to friggin' ask?

Greta *tsk-tsked*. "Cooper will be fine. It's a simple procedure."

He shook his head, sighed. "Tell that to anyone who's ever had his business cut off."

"Oh, Harry." His wife smiled, kissed his cheek. "The two of you will be lounging around watching reruns of James Bond tomorrow evening."

"You think so?" The thought of a scalpel near his private parts made him light-headed.

A gentle laugh, another kiss on his cheek. "I know so."

He slung an arm around Greta, leaned back against the leather of the couch cushions. What would she say if she discovered Cooper had crawled up on the couch last night? *How did he manage to get up there, Harry Blacksworth? Are you responsible for this?* And then, because he'd never hide a damn thing from her bordering on an untruth, he'd nod and admit he'd invited the dog because the poor guy was going under the knife the next morning. *Rules, Harry. We talked about this.* She'd follow it with a sigh and a shake of her blonde head. *This dog has four orthopedic beds and his own couch!*

"Harry?"

Her voice pulled him back, calmed him. What had he done all these years without her? No need to ponder a ridiculous question like that because he knew, hell yes, he did. He'd gotten into too damn much trouble and stayed there because nobody had the guts to call him on it. Not even Charlie who liked to talk about what he called Harry's *unused potential*, but what did that really mean? For a guy like Harry, he needed someone like Greta to kick him in the butt, tell him he wasn't king of the world. Yup, she'd done that all right, and then some. He pulled her closer, kissed her temple. "I don't know what I'd ever do without you."

"Nor I you, but if you sneak Cooper on this couch again, *he'll* be your new bed partner."

～

EMMA HALE LEARNED ABOUT MAGDALENA, New York, from a woman in her yoga class. When Paige mentioned her cousin left Philly for a small town in the Catskills where people helped each other through difficult times, and family was about more than blood, the idea intrigued Emma. According to Paige, the cousin had found happiness with a wife, two children, and a life that brought him peace, joy, contentment.

For a person who'd spent the last few years searching for peace, joy, contentment, *and* love—this town would be an opportunity to start over. Emma wanted out of the city that reminded her too much of the past and the man she needed to forget. Her therapist told her it wasn't the man who was the problem, but Emma's choice and expectations in men that created a continual upheaval of disappointment.

Maybe Emma *did* have skewed ideas about the perfect mate, and maybe that person should not be connected to another woman, even by separation. But when someone tells you his marriage is over, and the lengthy separation is necessary to ensure the children aren't scarred—why wouldn't you believe him? Should he be punished for being a good man, a respectable father? She'd believed the smiles, the *I love yous* and the *we will have a life together*, right up until he told her *Things have changed. My wife and I are giving it another go. I'm sorry. I'm sorry.* Sorry didn't matter, sorry didn't fix the gouge in her heart, the emptiness in her soul. She'd loved this man, rehabilitated his broken bones, healed his heart from the tragedy of a doomed marriage, and given him renewed hope that love and happily-ever-afters still existed. And what had she received in return? A twenty-second phone call that included words like *We never should have happened...you helped me through a difficult time...always be grateful...not going to work out...need to try and make the marriage work...*

Why did that always happen to her? The therapist said she loved too much, and perhaps it was the *idea* of love rather than the person that motivated her. Or, perhaps it was her desire to heal and fix not just a body but the whole person: mind, heart, soul. Was this true? Was Emma a healer who helped others at the cost to herself and her well being?

She didn't know, didn't want to know because she'd quit therapy when she decided to move to the town her yoga friend, Paige, had mentioned. Some might call it a whim or a wish, but the more Paige spoke of Magdalena, New York, the more Emma's interest and desire to live there grew. Emma kept her inquiries subtle, a comment here and there that would not indicate her purpose or her intention.

Do you really think Magdalena is the place to be?

Tell me about the people there.

So, your cousin has found true happiness?

And the unspoken curiosity she wondered about until the decision became final; *Will Magdalena make me happy? Will I find peace and joy and contentment there? Maybe even love?* Emma planned her move, investigated the possibility of physical therapy work, conducted a phone interview, and flew in for face-to-face interviews at Magdalena General Hospital. The town proved quaint, welcoming, and peaceful. The bed and breakfast where she stayed, owned and operated by proprietor and town mayor Mimi Pendergrass, was magical, a balm to her tired soul. Hope sprung in her heart once again when she received the job offer from Magdalena General Hospital, and on a crisp fall day, Emma loaded the car and headed to the small furnished bungalow Mimi had recommended.

Emma tried to forget the man who broke her heart and refused to believe the therapist's words about caring too much and imposing her own fantasies on people. Instead, she planned to heal those she could, open herself to new experiences...open herself to *love* again, and this time it would be with the right man. She would not end up like her mother, alone, afraid, desperate for a man to bring her happiness. Their father was long gone, suffocated by what some said was his wife's incessant dissatisfaction with life. Edgar William Hale had driven to the bowling alley one Thursday night and never returned, leaving nothing behind but a two-sentence note, *I can't take it anymore. Tell the girls I love them.*

How could a man who loved his children leave them? And what couldn't he take? Had Emma and her sister been too much responsibility? Her twelve-year-old brain could not understand how this could happen and had done what any child in her situation would do: she asked her mother.

Your father never cared about you girls.

If he cared, would he have left you?

He's gone and good riddance.

He never wanted you, did you know that?

On and on she went, scarring her older daughter with cruel words, making sure Emma knew her mother had *not* deserted them, though she could have. Emma tried to bring happiness into their gray existences, but it was impossible to make her mother see that life offered choices and opportunities. Norma Hale did not want to hear of either, counting herself a victim of circumstance, a single parent whose problems of money and discontent could be solved by the presence of a man. Any man. Except that was never true. Men came and went, taking what their mother offered until there was nothing left, not even her mother's delicate beauty. Perhaps that's what turned Emma into a fixer and a healer, a deliverer of hope and possibility, one who strived to help, no matter what.

It was the no-matter-what that skewed her perception of helping and healing. Emma believed in order to help and heal, she must immerse herself, body, heart, soul, into whatever or whomever needed her help.

Often it was a man.

Often it ended badly.

And that's what landed Emma in Magdalena General Hospital's physical therapy department, where after two months she'd gained the title of angel, savior, doer of good deeds. Was it the kind words bestowed, the physical therapy sessions, the bright smiles? Perhaps it was the motivational books she often provided her patients, along with the calm message that hope and determination could lead one to a path of healing. Some said it was the double chocolate chip cookies she brought to work, while others insisted it was the ethereal quality that clung to her like a halo.

Whatever it was, everyone noticed it.

Especially Gina Reed.

3

_____

ive weeks after the accident

F The man lying in the hospital-issue bed in the center of their living room was not the same one she'd married four years ago. This one was withdrawn, sullen, and not interested in a wife or her desire to help him. No, this Ben Reed preferred to dwell on his own misery and the misfortune attached to it. Gina had never been one for soft words, sharing, or expressing emotion. Ben had changed all that, made it easier for her to show she cared and to say the words attached to that caring. *I love you. I can't live without you. You live in my heart.* With him, she didn't hide her feelings or the deep love that owned her heart. *That* was the Ben Reed she'd married, the one she'd shared children, dreams, and a bed with...

Life was not always easy or predictable, and though she didn't want to admit or accept that fact, Gina knew deep down that no matter the lists or the attempts to control a situation, life was full of surprises, not all of them good. Christine called them challenges, said they made a person stronger, even when those challenges appeared insurmountable.

Like now. Ben didn't want to talk, nor did he want her to guide him through exercises or offers of advice on how to improve muscle tone, strength, and flexibility. No hang-in-there-it-will-get-better conversations or let's-be-grateful-for-what-we-have reminders, because he wasn't interested. Her husband wasn't *interested* in much other than sleeping or pretending to sleep, watching television, or reading car magazines. He'd refused visits from Cash and Nate, and even Alex and Ava couldn't draw more than a stingy smile from their father.

Christmas and New Year's had come and gone and with it, the hope that Ben would accept his injury, or at least show a hint of patience about it. Not Ben. He'd tolerated her physical therapy help for eight sessions and then told her she was his wife, *not* his therapist, and he wanted someone else. What to say to that? The staff had been sympathetic, some had even tried to humor her with stories of their own spouse's refusal to accept their help, but for a person who didn't share personal situations, this was humiliating. And it made her angry.

Still, she'd cared for enough patients to understand the psychology behind an injury like this, especially one that rendered a man like Ben incapable of performing many of the tasks he'd taken for granted: standing on his own, showering without the use of a chair, getting dressed, driving, fixing a meal...sleeping with his wife. There'd been no inquiries about when he could maneuver upstairs to their bed, the place he'd once called a *safe haven*. The hospital bed had become his island, and from the looks of their situation, he planned to stay there a while.

It was difficult to pretend life was normal with Ben sprawled out on the darn metal monster in the center of the living room where Alex used to play with his train set or watch his favorite television program. At least, their son was too young to understand his father's withdrawn state, or the occasional backlash of anger that spewed from those beautiful lips. At the moment, there was nothing beautiful about the man or his stubborn attitude. And while he might have told his current physical therapist he didn't need him anymore since Gina was taking over at home, that was such a lie. Ben hadn't done anything but lie in bed these past three days.

She would find a way to make him care again because Gina was a fixer who did not give up or give in. No matter the years or the joy that filled her days, she could not erase the pain of growing up in a house where beauty trumped intelligence and integrity was not a trait to be admired. Gina had survived years of loneliness, and she would *not* sit by and let the family she and Ben created or the love they shared be destroyed by the accident.

But how would she make him care and who could help her?

The answer presented itself two days later in the form of Emma Hale, the new physical therapist from Philly. There'd been a lot of talk about Emma, touting her as the new *Angel of Hope and Healing*. No one had ever called Gina that, but maybe because she was more of a no-nonsense-what-you-see-is-what-you-get type of therapist who didn't shower bright smiles and positivity as a conversation starter. Still, if Emma Hale could convince Ben to care about his therapy, then smiles and positivity were a welcome part of Gina's plan.

She approached Emma that afternoon, offered a smile and a quiet, "Do you have a minute? There's something I'd like to talk to you about."

"Sure, my next patient isn't scheduled until 2:00 p.m. How about we chat in the break room?"

Gina followed the tall, leggy blonde as they moved toward the break room. Fresh-faced beautiful with brown eyes and the deepest dimples Gina had ever seen, it wasn't difficult to understand how patients would not want to disappoint her. Add a can-do attitude and a chocolate chip cookie or two, and who wouldn't push through the muscle discomfort to get the number of repetitions completed? The whole town knew she'd come from Philly, but they didn't know much else. Did she have family back there? What had made her choose small-town life, and why Magdalena? People wondered but no one dared ask, at least not yet. But whispers laid odds it was more than the need to see open space and know her neighbors that called her here. They said a man could be involved—maybe a boyfriend, a fiancé, or an ex-husband. Others argued that wasn't it at all, that the young woman had grown tired of the frantic pace of city life and the strangers who would never become more than that. Those people said Emma Hale had arrived in their town to *find* a man and start a family.

Who knew what the truth was? It could be one or none, or a combination. Gina didn't care; as long as the woman helped her husband, that's all that mattered.

Emma pulled out a chair, eased onto it. Sadness clouded her dark eyes when she spoke. "How's your husband doing?" The whole department knew about Ben's accident, but what they didn't know was that the man they called charming, witty, a dream come true, had shut out his family and friends, choosing to spend time in self-pity and misery.

Talking about it would be tricky because there were only so many ways to avoid the truth. "He's recovering slowly…"

When Gina's voice wobbled, Emma leaned forward, said in a soft voice, "But?"

"But…" Gina sucked in a breath, forced out the words that could help her husband. "He's having a difficult time. I've had patients like him before, strong, capable, independent ones who don't accept imperfections or impairments, no matter how temporary."

"Oh. I see." Emma clasped Gina's hand, squeezed. "I've had a few patients like that myself. One was too smothered in his own misery to heal himself. It was a bad ending." She blinked, shook her head. "Lost his job, his marriage, his kids…"

"How sad."

"I still think about that patient, wonder what I might have done differently to help him. Healing is about so much more than muscles, tendons, and bones, and yet the mind-body-spirit correlation is often ignored."

Gina guessed the woman had a point, but she'd never felt it was right to dive into those areas, not unless someone asked, and even then, she'd do no more than dip a toe into the murkiness. But Emma didn't sound like she minded jumping right in and muddying the waters, no matter what lay beneath. "It's hard to stand by and watch."

Emma shrugged, worked up a smile. "Caring about someone means that sooner or later, you're going to get hurt. Still, it doesn't mean you close your heart, no matter how deep the pain, because that's not living." She eased her hand from Gina's, sat back. "I came to this town to find peace and maybe, if I'm lucky, a chance for a little joy."

What did that mean other than this woman knew about hurt and sadness? Did it matter? Once Gina knew her better, maybe Emma would share her story, and perhaps Gina could introduce her to Christine, Tess, and Bree. Her friends were strong, capable women who would be almost as grateful as Gina if Emma could make Ben care again, show him life was still good, no matter the obstacles or challenges that stood before him. "Would you be willing to work with Ben? He's not..." The next part was painful to admit, but she had to say it. "He's not really interested in working with me, and I get it. How many times have we heard family members are the worst in rehab and you should never work with your spouse unless you're looking for a disaster?"

"Too many, and probably all true." Emma's face lit up like the sun on a cloudless day. "Family is difficult because we're too close. I'd like to help, just tell me what I can do."

"I'll get the okay from the department for you to provide in-home treatment and update you on where he was with his sessions, and then you can get started." *And Ben can get his life back.* Hope and sadness squeezed Gina's heart. He was such a good man with so much to offer, and yet he'd shut down since the accident. She understood how a person whose body operated like a performance machine could grow despondent when that body failed, but he was so much more than muscle and brawn, and maybe Emma could show him that—the sooner, the better. Ben had quit therapy at the hospital where people could gawk and see how weak he'd become. He didn't admit this was the reason, but he didn't have to, because Gina already knew.

BEN BLINKED HIS EYES OPEN, tried to focus on the vision in front of him. What the hell? He blinked again, stared. The vision was a woman: tall, blonde, dark-eyed. He scrubbed a hand over his face, narrowed his gaze. "Who are you?" He took in the mint-green polo shirt and black slacks, the hesitant smile. "Did my wife send you?" The woman ignored his question, placed a hand on the bed rail, moved closer.

"Hello, Ben. I'm Emma Hale. Gina and I work together." She paused, offered up a wide smile. "I'm from Philly. I've only been here a few months, but I like it. Cozy, inviting..."

He should be ticked that she was in his house but talk of Philly had him curious. "Philly, huh?" *Philly was a lifetime ago.*

A nod of her blonde braid. "Yes. Good old Philly." The sigh followed, a wistful "That was some place."

Visions of frenetic activity and sensory overload burst in his head, simmered. "It was," he admitted as the remembrance smoothed out to include other memories: the restaurants, the music, his motorcycle...

"Unless you've experienced the place, you can't quite understand it. There's something about the mood and the energy that gets inside you. And the food? Oh, what I wouldn't give for a Philly cheesesteak or a slice of pizza." Laughter spilled from her lips, swirled to the hospital bed, pulled him in. "Not the stuff other people call pizza, but a real Philly slice."

Ben smiled, something he hadn't done in a long time. "You've got that right, though there's a guy in town who does a pretty good imitation. Actually, he's just a kid, but can he cook. He's the chef at the Italian restaurant here." He paused, scratched his jaw. The three-week-old beard proved more annoyance than anything, but he hadn't been interested in personal grooming or listening to his wife's comments about *joining the human race* with a shave.

"I'd like to try it, but I'm not sure I'll be persuaded."

Ben's smile spread. "Hold judgment until you've tasted Jeremy's pizza." He shook his head, let out a sigh. "How a guy with that kind of talent ever thought he'd stay a cop just to please his old man is plain crazy."

"You'd be surprised what children will do to please their parents. Or what people will do to please each other, even if it's the last thing they want to do." She clutched the bed rail, her voice drifting. "But what happens when they wake up and realize they're doing it all for someone else? That they don't even want *that thing*...that relationship? I've known people who say marriage is an attempt to control another person, that if you really care about someone, a piece of paper isn't necessary." Sadness spread across her pale face. "They say commitment is about what's in the heart and a piece of paper doesn't stop a cheater."

"Boy, whoever 'they' is doesn't think much of marriage." He'd bet it was a guy. Hadn't he been known to toss out clever phrases about not getting tied down, marriage as a control mechanism, crap like that? Big, tough-guy stuff, but that was after the divorce and maybe that's how he'd ended up divorced. Of course, back then, he kept his real feelings to himself, but that was all pre-Gina. Once she came along, so did the opening up and sharing, though right now he and his wife weren't sharing much of anything.

"No, I guess they don't think much of marriage."

The brightness in those dark eyes said she might be talking about someone who meant a lot to her, like a guy. Had she fallen for someone who didn't want to take the plunge into marriage and had given her the old what's-the-point-in-a-piece-of-paper crap? He'd bet she had. "Hey, sorry about the guy, and if it matters, he sounds like a jerk."

A shrug, a soft smile. "Thank you." Those dark eyes glistened. "But I'm the one who's supposed to make *you* feel better."

"Then let's talk about anything other than the real reason you're here." Ben motioned to the brace on his left knee. "How about we discuss the Eagles or the Phillies? I'm guessing if you lived in Philly, you had to cheer one of those teams."

"Both actually."

"Ah, both. I figured you for a sports fan."

"I'm a sports fan who used to be a sports player." She lifted her arm and feigned a volleyball serve. "I broke my arm skateboarding when I was a sophomore in college, and six months later, I broke my leg skiing." A wince, followed by a deep breath. "Guess I shouldn't have tried that last jump. I was miserable. I mean, miserable. I thought my world had ended. The volleyball scholarship I'd earned was gone, the boyfriend I trained with—gone."

Okay, so maybe he wasn't the only person who'd had his share of bad luck. "Tough break."

"Tough break?" She laughed. "You could call it that. I hated everybody, even myself, but then one day I decided I could spend my life crying about what I'd lost, or I could start rebuilding my life, maybe make it better."

He pictured a younger version of Emma Hale, angry, disappointed that life had cheated her out of the future she'd wanted. But there was something to be said for a person who could push through it and find her way out of a dark place. And being a kid? She must be made of strong stuff:

resilience, determination, perseverance. "So, you might have given up volleyball, but it's obvious you've done something." The long leanness, athletic stance, and high-end tennis shoes said *runner.* "You're a runner."

The blonde braid swung against her shoulder when she shook her head. "Not anymore. Time and too much pavement caught up with me. These days it's yoga, spinning, and dance classes. I swim, too." She eyed him as if assessing his ability level. "Swimming would definitely help you. Maybe we should add that to your program."

Ah, she was a clever one. "You mean the program I haven't agreed to yet? That one?"

Her lips twitched. "Yes, that one." Emma leaned toward him, her voice slipping two octaves. "The one you're going to agree to because you're thinking if a kid could get past the anger and rework her dreams, surely a man like you could."

This time, Ben didn't try to pretend he didn't know what she was doing. "You enjoy sparring, don't you? Try to appeal to my tough-guy mentality, see if you can get me to cave?" He eyed her. "Nice tactic, but I'm still not interested in therapy. Look, I know what I need to do." That was BS, but he did not want to be bothered with the nags and the demands. He'd figure it out in his own time, without anyone seeing what he could and couldn't do. It was damn embarrassing to get winded crutch-walking six feet, and forget the heavy weights. Bad enough to admit he'd turned into a wimp. Others, including his wife, might guess at his difficulties, but unless they *witnessed* the failed attempts, they'd still only be a guess.

"Okay, fine." She backed away, eased onto the rocker he'd given Gina when Alex was born and placed her hands on the armrests. "You don't want therapy. So, what's your favorite restaurant in Philly?"

Ben didn't realize how much he missed normal conversation that was not about his injury or his recovery. With Gina, it was *always* about both, same with the friends and well-wishers he'd been refusing to see. At some point, a guy just wanted to feel like a person again, talk about football, Philly cheesesteaks, sports cars, and the dream conversation that he absolutely could not have with his wife—motorcycles. Who would have guessed Emma knew about V-Twins and changing out exhaust pipes to get the perfect rumble? Most people would call a person crazy for replacing brand-new stock pipes before the bike rolled off the showroom floor, just because the sound wasn't quite right. If Gina knew people did that, she'd call them crazy, foolish, *and* wasteful. Of course, he and Gina didn't discuss bikes at all, unless she caught him staring at the corner of the garage where his Road King sat, protected with a gray cover like a shroud. Then she had plenty to say with comments about *taking up space* and *what's the point?*

Emma wanted to talk bikes, had once traveled The Blue Ridge Parkway on the back of a Harley Electra Glide. *Peaceful, breathtaking, spiritual*, she'd called it. *More calming than a yoga retreat*. Ben laughed when she confessed to missing the motorcycle much more than the old boyfriend. That confession dovetailed with one of his own: he missed riding. A lot.

"So, why don't you ride?"

Good question. "I...kind of made a deal with Gina when we got married." He picked at a piece of crusted egg on his T-shirt. "She's not big on motorcycles; hates them. So..."

"So, you gave up something you love—" she paused, her voice downshifting "—because you love her more."

"Right." That pretty much summed it up.

"But couldn't you have both? Wouldn't Gina want you to do what you loved?"

How to answer that? His wife wanted him to do what he loved provided it met her standards and passed *her* safety-and-low-risk test. "It's not that simple. Gina has particular concerns, and it's my job not to magnify them."

The look on Emma's face said she didn't understand. Or maybe that look said she *did* understand and couldn't believe what he'd just admitted. "Would she really expect you to sacrifice that happiness?" And then, the zinger that spun him around and started the chaos that would later become his life. "Isn't marriage about compromise and making each other happy?"

Ben forced a laugh. "Spoken by someone who's not married. Of course, it's about compromise and happiness, but the real trick is knowing what's negotiable and what's off the table." He shrugged, considered the topic of the motorcycle. "And riding a motorcycle again is pretty much off the table. I count it a win she hasn't strong-armed me to sell it." That he couldn't do, and maybe Gina realized it because she'd never straight out asked him.

"Strong-armed?" Emma shook her head, her voice sad. "Maybe that's why I'm not married. I don't think I'd want anyone to strong-arm me." A pause, a wistful "I'd want him to understand the importance of my choices, and if we didn't agree, I'd want him to accept that, and be okay with it." She offered a half smile. "Really okay, not a lukewarm I'll-let-you-do-this okay." Another pause. "Wouldn't you want that?"

Her words swirled through his brain, made him wonder if Gina shouldn't be less demanding on the motorcycle stance. Still, she'd given him so much: love, a home, a family.

Purpose. Could he not give her the peace of knowing he wouldn't get on the bike again? Show her by selling it? The thought squeezed his gut. Why couldn't Gina be as understanding about his need to ride as Emma? Hell, if a woman he'd just met could tell, shouldn't his wife be able to see? Another gut squeeze. Maybe Gina did see and chose to ignore it. Ben let out a sigh. Maybe Gina saw everything, and it didn't matter. "It's not that simple."

"It should be. Shouldn't it?"

Later, he would recognize the moment he let selfishness and ego crowd out love and common sense. "Yeah, it should be." Even when it wasn't...

Emma eased out of the rocking chair, moved toward him, her smile brighter than an afternoon sun in July. "Why not let me help you get back to your old self, so maybe one day you'll get back on that bike. It could be that simple." She reached out, placed a hand on his forearm. "You can do this, Ben. You deserve it, but you have to let me help you. You don't belong in a hospital bed, reading car magazines and watching the clock. You've got a whole life to live, and you'll come back stronger and better than ever." Her voice dipped, spilled with a sweetness that sucked him right in, faster than the ant traps he'd set in the kitchen last spring. "You deserve to get on that bike again, and I'm going to help you."

It would take two more visits, a plateful of chocolate chip cookies, and a whole lot of talk about bikes, performance cars, and the Philadelphia Eagles for Ben to admit maybe he could use a little help transitioning from injured reserve to suited-up-and-ready-to-get-back-in-the-game status. A football analogy worked for him, except it hadn't been his. Emma had been the one to toss it out like a penalty flag after a holding call. And the thought of getting on the bike again?

Well, that was the Super Bowl ring, and while he'd have to convince Gina, he couldn't think about that right now because what he needed at this moment was a goal and that bike was his goal.

"Will you let me help you, Ben?"

He'd just eaten another chocolate chip cookie, his third, and had a slight sugar buzz going. Buzz or not, he should have told her "thanks but no thanks" and then he should have called Gina and told her he was ready to start therapy again—real therapy with her help, not the BS stuff he'd been doing on his own. But part of him wanted to show her that she didn't always know what he needed, and that marriage should be about compromise, not caving, and maybe that's what he'd done when he'd given up the bike. Maybe he'd caved because he'd been so damn in love and desperate for her approval, but was that right? If she really loved him, should she expect him to become a different person? He'd given up the sports car and parked the bike. What was next? No, damn it, no. Ben snatched another cookie, met Emma's gaze, and said, "When do we start?"

4

"I hear you've got a new sidekick." Nate slid into a chair, looked around. "Where is he? Greta said you've been busy logging in walking miles, vet appointments, poop patrol, and deciding on the perfect orthopedic bed for the newest Blacksworth."

"Go to hell." Harry shook his head, handed Nate a glass of water and chugged down half of his own. "I didn't know it was going to be this much work, and either the guy's got a lot of energy or I'm getting old."

Nate laughed. "You'll never be old, Harry." Another laugh, this one deeper than the last. "Even when you're eighty-five. It's just not who you are."

That made Harry perk up. Damn straight on that one. A person was only as old as he let himself be, and Harry Blacksworth was not going to get old. Nope. He planned to copy a page right out of Pop Benito's too-busy-to-get-old playbook. "It's all in the outlook, right? Maybe it's not me at all, maybe it's Cooper." Harry leaned forward, said in a low voice, "That guy is something else. He runs like a gazelle, flat out, ears back, so much speed. Never saw anything like it. The vet says he might look like a black Lab, but he's got pointer in him, too. That's why he's got the nose. You know that guy can sniff out a mole? I watched him the other day, tracking a pattern in the grass like nobody's business. He found two mice in the garage and if he hadn't been on a leash, that would have been the end of them. Same with the squirrels in the backyard. You should see him eyeball them like he's just waiting for them to make a mistake."

"Sounds like he's following his instincts." Nate raised a brow. "You know, like being a dog who likes road kill rather than a gourmet feast."

Harry fought the heat creeping up his neck, splashing to his cheeks. "Did Christine tell you about that?" More heat splashing his cheeks. "What's wrong with letting your dog taste-test his meal choices? I thought it made sense; less waste and you figure it out all at once."

A shake of the man's head told Harry he wasn't buying his BS. "You had Jeremy create meals for the animal, Harry. Sirloin, lamb, turkey, and salmon. Who does that? And why?"

It sounded like a good idea, but other than Jeremy, who would create a meal for a fish if he could, everybody else thought he was nuts. "I nixed the sirloin, lamb, and turkey," he said. "Decided on the salmon and Jeremy tossed in sweet potato." Pause and then, what the hell, might as well admit the truth. "The vet said dogs don't have palates that require change and I'm causing the boy's bowels more harm than good by switching every few days." He shrugged, thought of Cooper's stinky messes. "I just wanted to give him choices because from those fly bites behind his ears and the ribs sticking out, I'd say he didn't have many of those." Harry dragged a hand over his face, thought of the tragedy he'd learned of yesterday. "The dog's afraid of fire, Nate. I don't mean a bonfire, I'm talking about a candle. Greta lit one of those aromatherapy ones she favors, and the poor guy flew out of the room and hid. AJ found him in the laundry room, hunkered in a corner, shaking. What could have happened to make him do that, huh?"

Nate shrugged. "No idea, but you need to relax so the dog relaxes."

"I know that, but *I'm* it, Nate. Me. Solo. Nobody else. Sure, the kids and even Greta will help, but that dog depends on me. What if I screw up, leave brownies on the counter or chicken bones? He'll get into them and what if he croaks?" He shook his head, blew out a long sigh and wished he'd diluted his drink with scotch instead of straight-up water. "You know I'm no good in emergency situations; look what happened when Greta fell in the pool." He swiped a hand over his forehead, tried to block out memories of the day he almost lost his wife. "If AJ hadn't taken over and called 9-1-1, Greta might not have made it. Damn, but I should have turned the dog over to a shelter so somebody who knew what they were doing could adopt him, not a wannabe do-gooder loser like me."

"Yeah, that's you, a wannabe do-gooder loser." Nate pushed his empty glass toward Harry. "How about you fill our glasses with some of the good stuff and then tell me what's really going on." He slipped Harry a smile, added, "And I want to meet Cooper."

Harry grinned. "Good stuff coming up, and he's in the basement watching TV with AJ. I'll go get him." He should have known Nate would see through his hand-wringing BS and want real answers. Harry wanted real answers, too, but he didn't know why he'd become obsessed with a scrawny, fly-bitten mutt who was afraid of candles. He called for Cooper from the top of the basement stairs and seconds later, the dog bounded up the steps toward him, mouth open, tail wagging like Harry was king of his world—which he was. "Hey, boy, I've got somebody I want you to meet. He's a real pain in the butt, but a straight shooter, loyal, and he's family. Kind of like you." He pointed at Nate, laughed. "Go check him out."

Cooper ran toward Nate, who held out a hand for the dog to sniff. Four sniffs and a lot of tail-wagging later, Nate eased a hand along the dog's back and said in a gentle voice, "You're a handsome boy, aren't you?" More tail wagging, a nuzzle against Nate's other hand. "Loyal, too, from what I hear. How about you train your father to pick up after himself, so you can't get into brownies or chicken bones?"

The dog's back end wiggled, and his mouth opened in what Lizzie called a doggy smile. Nate kept talking nonsense about training Harry and teaching him about consistency and rules—the two essentials in parenting. Cooper leaned against Nate's thigh, slid to the floor, and rested his head against his new buddy's shoe. "Damn, but you have a way with dogs."

Nate slid him a look. "I've known my share of mongrels. Hell, I *was* one until Christine tamed me."

That made Harry laugh. "Isn't that the truth! My niece can make a pig look like a prince if she sets her mind to it."

The man raised a brow. "So, I'm a pig who turned into a prince? Not sure I like that comparison." He ran a hand along Cooper's side, pulled a contented sigh from the dog. "How about we skip the BS and you tell me what's really behind the obsession you'll screw up with this guy?"

It took three gulps of scotch before Harry spilled the

truth he hadn't realized until a few seconds ago. "Okay, here you go. The way I see it, I've never been responsible for anyone except myself, and look how I turned out? When Charlie died, I stepped in and tried to help Chrissie, but I could have done better."

"You did your best, considering the circumstances." Nate's dark eyes shifted to black, his gaze narrowed. "You did more than her father ever did."

"I guess. Still, I was no savior. And then there's Greta and the kids. She's my rock and if I get close to messing up with the kids, she'll yank me back in line." He let out a long sigh. "There's real comfort in that."

"Sure there is." Nate sipped his drink, nodded. "It's called teamwork and commitment and once you have it, you depend on it."

Spoken from a man who'd spent a lot of years on his own, trusting no one, holding his secrets close, his insecurities closer. Not that a man like Nate Desantro had a boatload of insecurities like Harry did, but the man wasn't without a few. "You got it, but Greta made it clear I was on my own with the dog, but I didn't think she really meant it. Hell, I figured she'd fall for the guy like I did and by day three, she'd be oohing and aahing all over him." He shook his head, frowned. "Didn't happen. By day three, she told me if one of the kids stepped in Cooper's messes again, I was cleaning their shoes, and then she told me to get a plan because she was not going to be part of it. Did I know I had to go hunting for dog crap every six hours? I did it, though, and I came up with a strategy, because I was not going to let the dog or the kids down. And once the plan was in place, I figured Greta would buy in and help, but she's not budging on the you-brought-it-you-own-it concept. At least she supported me when he got his business taken care of...you know..."

"I heard you had sympathy pains." Nate coughed, smiled. "Did you think you were getting neutered, too?"

Talk of a scalpel in anybody's private area, especially his, made Harry queasy. "I pictured it, sure. What guy wouldn't?"

Nate set his glass on the table, said in a firm voice, "This guy. Why would you do that, Harry? Neutering an animal is a responsible decision."

He nodded. "I know...but do you think the guy suffered? I mean, who knows if he was in pain? He didn't act like it when he came home, but who's to say? I think the pillow and the blanket helped, and I think he liked me lying on the floor with him." Harry chuckled. "We fell asleep watching 007."

"I didn't know Cooper liked James Bond."

The look that accompanied those words said Harry was two shades shy of crazy. Well, how about three shades? Might as well ask the question he'd wondered about since agreeing to get his dog snipped. "Do you think he misses his *package*?"

Long pause and then "No, Harry, I don't." Another pause, this one longer than the first. "Did you ever think about talking to a dog person? Someone who *has* a dog? Like Cash maybe? He'd be a good one, could tell you all about Henry, his and Tess's firstborn." He nodded, rubbed his jaw. "That dog came into their lives when they needed him, so I guess you could say they rescued each other. Maybe Cooper reminds you a little too much of yourself, ever think of that?"

Ding, ding, ding. Of course, he'd thought of it. Harry wasn't into philosophical mumbo jumbo, but hadn't he been a mongrel, roaming and untamed, not housebroken, afraid of the fire of commitment? Hell, yes! A big sigh, followed by a bigger gulp of scotch. "Maybe you're onto something."

That made Nate laugh. "Maybe, huh?"

"Okay, you nailed it. Cooper's me in dog form and I can't screw this up because in some bizarre way, he stands for where I've been and how far I've come."

"Huh. How about that?" Nate lifted his glance, saluted him. "Harry Blacksworth, philosopher and man of introspection. You got this, Harry, so follow your gut and relax about the dog...and talk to Cash. He'll set you straight."

~

EIGHT WEEKS after the accident

Ben Reed was the perfect blend of determination, perseverance, and muscle, all wrapped up in an athlete's body. It had been three weeks since Emma started working with him. While she'd never doubted the man's ability, it was Ben's attitude and drive that propelled him toward recovery. Commitment had been key; once he'd chosen to get his body back, he'd been full-on unstoppable in his desire to regain his former self. But which former self did he want back? The married one with two children who lived in the suburbs and had a motorcycle he didn't ride parked in the garage? Or the one who'd lived a spontaneous, daring life that included a city with more than two restaurants and a motorcycle he *did* ride?

It was difficult to tell whether Gina was pleased with the results because she asked a lot of questions, ones that almost sounded as though she didn't agree with Emma's therapy plan. But the results were hard to ignore. After three weeks under Emma's care and guidance, Ben's strength and mobility had increased, he was almost at full weight bearing, and the man even smiled. A lot. It wouldn't be much longer before she could get him on the exercise bike...

Yes, he could have achieved some success on his own, but the results would not have been stellar. Emma drove him to the hospital's recreation center where he swam four times a week, and with a little coaxing, she joined in. How could a person refuse someone with such determination? The smile didn't hurt either.

But perhaps what changed the most each day was the man's attitude toward his injury and the outcome. Ben told her he didn't plan to just sit and watch his life go by, that at thirty-nine, he still had goals and a life to live. She agreed, encouraged him to expand those goals and live that life. Who knew what that meant? Did it matter? Why should he be limited by age and a family?

Should people not be encouraged to be individuals, with their own thoughts and their own dreams? She and Ben had this discussion, and he'd been surprised with her comment that couples could be together while still leading separate lives. In fact, she'd stated she believed it was necessary for a healthy relationship.

If a husband wants to travel to Alaska by himself and see the glaciers, why shouldn't he?

If the wife decides to take cooking classes in Sorrento... Should the husband say no?

Why should there be boundaries?

Why should one person try to control another?

Why can't a husband and wife live together, respect one another's opinions, give them the freedom and the encouragement to do what they want to do?

And then, the comment that made his brows pinch

together seconds before they smoothed out and his lips pulled into that slow smile she'd come to recognize as happiness.

And why shouldn't a husband be allowed to head out on his motorcycle to the Bourbon Trail, or the famous Route 66, maybe even Sturgis, if the burn is in his soul? Emma had promised Gina she'd get results and heal Ben, and that's exactly what she intended to do. However, Gina might not agree with Emma's methods, and maybe that was the problem. After the third meeting to obtain Ben's therapy status, where Gina drilled Emma with questions, concerns, even suggestions, it had become obvious that Ben's wife needed to remain on the sidelines and let Emma make the assignments. How could she achieve success if she became Gina's mouthpiece? Ben would resent it and he wouldn't trust her. It was the trust that mattered most; once that was gone, she might as well sign off and tell him she couldn't be his therapist.

Gina agreed in principle, but not in practice. That much was obvious from the tightness around her mouth and the spark in those dark eyes when she asked *You don't want me to ask anything about my husband's progress? I'm not sure I'm comfortable with that.*

No, Gina would not be comfortable with it, but then for a person who, according to Ben, wanted to control all situations and outcomes, Gina wouldn't be comfortable with anything short of a video recorder in the room where she could observe Ben's progress and the nuances involved. Emma let Gina know she would not continue working with Ben unless Gina relinquished all control. *It's about trust, isn't it? Ben has to trust me, and I have to give him that trust. I can't tell him you're not involved when you are. He needs time and the opportunity to come back from this injury with new energy, new strength, new results.*

That's how she got Gina to agree, and that's how she got Ben Reed to commit to success.

Trust was essential, and Ben needed to trust her in everything. Emma didn't stop to consider that her method of massaging situations and reworking the truth might not fit into the category of trust and might be a deal breaker for a stand-up guy like Ben Reed. None of that mattered but getting him to believe in himself *and* her.

Magdalena was indeed a cozy town, full of generosity and community. It was a place where people believed family was not always about blood relatives. Didn't she hear the stories of the Blacksworths and the Desantros? And what about the old Italian man, Angelo Benito, the one who guided the town and had been dubbed the "Godfather of Magdalena"? Emma liked to think she might belong here one day, that people might draw her in and welcome her as family.

The shops in town were different from the ones in Philly where there were so many choices and so many people. In Philly, a person could choose from dozens of places to have a haircut and manicure. In Magdalena, there were exactly two: Kit's Primp and Polish and Natalie's Salon & Spa. Emma stayed away from the first because she didn't like the name and ventured into the second because she did. Natalie Trimble was beautiful, mysterious, alluring. What was her story? Why did she try to hide her attractiveness behind clothing that was a size too big? Emma wondered about this as Natalie worked on her hands. The woman had gentle, efficient fingers that knew how to massage, buff, and trim.

"So, tell me about yourself? Are you from here? How did you get into nails and facials?"

Natalie kept her head bent, but Emma didn't miss the two-second hesitation before she answered. "Yes, I'm from Magdalena. And I guess I always loved the idea of making a woman feel good about herself."

Why the dip in her voice, the hint of sadness that said there was more? "That's a worthy cause. I think it's important to help other people."

The woman inched her dark gaze to Emma's, nodded. "I hear you're helping Ben Reed."

Mention of her new patient made Emma smile. "I am. He's a model patient, but then wouldn't you expect him to be?"

"I hope he'll feel more like his old self soon. Everybody's wishing for it."

"His old self? I don't know what that was, but I can promise he'll be better than his old self." Oh yes, the new Ben Reed would be fearless. "Did you know he's got a motorcycle in his garage and is desperate to ride it, but won't because of his wife?"

The nail technician cleared her throat, bit her bottom lip. "Gina's trying to protect the family by encouraging Ben to be safe."

"Safe? What's safe? The man fell from a ladder in his garage when he was trying to retrieve Christmas decorations. In Philly, he was a cop, a motorcycle rider, a lover of fast cars and danger, but a plastic snowman took him down. There is no safe and there is no protect." Emma leaned forward, her voice filled with the same emotion she used when she told Ben, "There's only living and not living."

"You mean breathing and doing whatever he wants, even if it jeopardizes his family? I don't agree. People make choices when they get married and decide to have children.

Those choices can't be about the next feel-good activity. They've got to mean something; they've got to be about the family and the relationship or what's the point? If a person does whatever he wants whenever he wants with whomever he wants—" her voice spilled a conviction that matched the fierceness of that dark gaze "—then the relationship is doomed."

Emma glanced at Natalie's wedding ring, shrugged. "If that works for you, then fine, but I wouldn't marry someone who tried to control me. I'd expect mutual consideration and that person would have the opportunity and the ability to do whatever he wanted. But, he'd be happy enough with me that he wouldn't *want* to..."

Natalie Trimble's lips pulled into a frown. "You mean you'd be enough for him? Your presence would consume him, and he'd never think about anything else because your brightness would obliterate the need?" Seconds after the words escaped, she apologized. "I'm sorry, I should not have said that. It's just that I don't want to see Ben and Gina get hurt. They belong together." Her voice dipped, shifted with feeling. "They've always belonged together."

Did they belong together? Maybe. And maybe Gina should let Ben be who he was and accept him instead of trying to change or control him. If she could do that, it would either strengthen the marriage or destroy it. If the first happened it was meant to be, and if the second happened, then...

5

Nine weeks after the accident

They called her an angel, a miracle worker sent from heaven to do the good Lord's work, instill hope, heal bodies, believe. Passion mixed with purpose and a refusal to quit or concede, that's what people said about Emma Hale.

Did you know she helped a paralyzed man walk again?

I heard he was blind and paralyzed. Did she help him see again, too?

I don't know, but it wouldn't surprise me.

She's an angel.

Magdalena is truly blessed.

Ben Reed sure is lucky to have her help.

She'll pull him through, make him whole again, you watch and see...

Who wouldn't heal with a miracle worker like that?

She's an angel...

What they didn't know and wouldn't know until it was too late was that everyone had a past, even those who wanted to pretend they didn't. And when that past intersected with the present, it could get messy—real messy. But for now, all they knew about the stunning physical therapist from Philly was what she told them and what they guessed.

Desperation makes a logical person set aside reason and grasp for hope, no matter the form. Gina Reed had never been one to run after gimmicks or unsubstantiated claims. She'd preferred options with a solid foundation that while not delivering earth-shattering rewards, would keep her safe, her life stable. Ben Reed had been the one choice based on emotion and heart and she'd never regretted it. Emma Hale was her second, but four weeks after hiring her to help Ben, Gina had doubts.

And the beginning of what felt an awful lot like regret.

Gina had once read that people walk into your life when you need them most, even if you don't understand that you need them. This was a difficult concept to understand because she'd never been one to rely on others, not her family, her friends, her business associates. The only person she'd ever relied on had been her husband, but since the accident, he hadn't been interested in anything but sinking in his own misery.

Until Emma Hale took over his therapy.

Hope became nebulous and uncertain in the days that followed. What did that word mean anyway? That you should believe in the possibility of a decent outcome, unless and until there was a change in the constant? Say a husband who fell off a ladder and no longer desired his wife as a partner, a therapist, a friend? *What happened to hope then?* Did he find someone else who offered him a newer, shinier version of the old hope? And what about the wife? What happened to *her* hope? Did it lay fractured, beaten and bruised with disappointment, die a slow death, or was the end a mercy killing so swift you never saw it coming?

Gina's life had downshifted from a husband, two children, and a bright future to a questionable husband, two children, and a not-so-shiny future. All because she'd insisted he retrieve the rest of the Christmas decorations in the attic along with that silly plastic snowman. If not for that, Ben wouldn't have fallen off the ladder, broken a bone, upended their lives. He would not have grown more distant, made her question his commitment to her, to their marriage.

Jealousy threatened to take over when she thought of Emma Hale working with Ben, but she refused to let emotion crowd out logic. The woman had been the perfect candidate to help Ben recover: well-qualified, stellar recommendations, a pristine education. So what if the woman was fresh-faced beautiful with dark eyes and a toned body from hours of physical fitness? And if her clothing hugged her body, helped onlookers imagine what lay beneath? So what?

None of that mattered because this woman was giving Ben back his life.

Gina had not considered this same woman might also take huge chunks of Ben's life for herself, but as the weeks passed and Ben grew more distant and argumentative, the possibility surfaced, settled in her brain. Of course, she never put thought to sound because it was only a feeling, not a knowing based on proof. But the feeling switched to possibility, which turned to probability the day another person shared those same concerns...someone who knew all about stealing men, even if the stealing *and* the men were relegated to a past life.

That someone was Natalie Servetti Trimble, the cousin who'd slept with Gina's first boyfriend, almost torn apart

Nate and Christine Desantro's marriage, destroyed too many relationships, and thought she had a right to whomever she wanted. Until she met mild-mannered accountant Robert Trimble, married him, had a baby boy named Dominic. Gone were the pounds of makeup, the low-cut tops, the second-skin outfits. If a newcomer entered Magdalena, he'd never believe the woman who favored a pale blush, sheer lip gloss, and "comfortable" clothing had been the sex-toy for too many of the town's men.

While past was past and relatives couldn't be erased, they could be avoided, and that's what Gina had done for a lot of years. But now the woman stood in the hospital parking lot, buried in a parka and snow boots, bracing against the cold February winds. "We need to talk," she said, rubbing her gloved hands together. "I wanted to call you, but I didn't have your number and I didn't want to ask your mother for it."

Good call on that one. Marie Servetti would interrogate her niece until she extracted information and her methods wouldn't be kind *or* empathetic. Still, what could Natalie have to say to Gina? Nothing she'd want to hear. She clicked open the car door and said, "Thanks for not calling my mother, but you shouldn't have come here. I doubt we have anything to talk about."

Natalie stepped forward, frowned. "Yes, we do." She clutched the hood of her parka with a gloved hand. "It's about Emma Hale."

"What about her?" Mention of the woman who had more access to her husband these days than she did put her on alert.

Natalie pointed at the car. "I'm freezing. Can we talk inside?"

Gina hesitated, considered which was worse: spending

time with Natalie or not knowing what she had to say about Emma. The latter won out. "Okay, but just for a minute." Natalie opened the door, eased inside. The woman would be beautiful in coveralls. So would Emma Hale. Thoughts of the other physical therapist's lean and toned body made Gina scowl. Looks and a beautiful body weren't everything, but some days Gina wished she'd known what it was like—even for a few days.

"I've seen people like Emma before..." A pause, a clearing of throat followed by "I've *been* Emma." Natalie clasped her gloved hands in her lap, dark eyes bright. "There's a look about them when they're after a man. That look says I'm coming to get you and I will do anything to have you."

Gina stared at her cousin, wondered how she'd made such a determination about Ben's therapist. "You sound pretty sure about this. Care to expand?" Had Natalie seen or heard something about Emma? Were Gina's random imaginings true? Were the sleepless nights for good reason and not the manic state of a woman who'd begun to doubt her own marriage?

A shake of that dark head and the words that made Gina uneasy. "She's been coming into the shop: facials, mani-pedis, waxing. When I heard who she was, I mentioned Ben and how we all hoped he'd be back to his old self soon, and she said he'd be better than his old self and you shouldn't keep him from doing what he loved."

"What he loved?" How was she keeping him from doing that? All she wanted was for him to get healthy, so they could get back to the way they were—happy.

Natalie shot her a look, said in a quiet voice, "I guess he misses riding his motorcycle."

That damn motorcycle. "Did he say that?" When Natalie

didn't answer, Gina looked away. "I see. Well, I'm sorry his world has been such a disappointment." She blinked hard, refusing to give in to tears.

"Please don't think that. Ben loves you, anybody can see that."

Anybody? If it were no longer obvious to Gina, then the only reason others still believed it was because they hadn't been around the not-so-happy couple since the accident. Trauma could cause a lot of damage to a relationship, especially when one of the parties refuses to admit there *is* a problem. Gina sucked in a breath, wished she could turn off the emotion and focus on the analytical side of her brain, but with Ben, that was impossible. How did a person rely on pure logic when her heart beat for the other person? And how did a person remain logical, when that heart was aching?

"Gina? Did you hear me? Ben loves you." Pause, a softer "Don't ever forget that. I told her when people get married they don't make choices that put each other or the family at risk. The choices they make are *for* each other, based on love, respect, and trust. If it's just about finding the next feel-good activity, then the relationship is doomed."

Who would have thought Natalie Servetti would be a champion for marriage, husbands, and family? Certainly not Gina, who'd suffered nothing but grief and animosity from her cousin. But maybe Natalie really *had* changed... "Thank you for telling me."

Natalie offered a tiny smile. "You're welcome. It's the least I could do." She cleared her throat. "There's more, though. She's been in a few times and each visit, she gets chummier, like she thinks we should be best buddies." Her brows pinched together as though she were picturing the conversation. "The other day, she started talking about Philly again, so I asked why she left and would she move back. She didn't give me a straight answer but talked about following your path and staying true to yourself. What's that supposed to mean?"

"It means she's avoiding the question."

"Right. She's definitely holding out on her reason for leaving Philly."

"No doubt."

"She told me she almost fell for some guy who'd been her patient, but the way she said it, there was no almost." Natalie heaved a sigh. "The look on her face and the pain in her voice said she was in deep and the guy didn't feel the same way." Pause, another sigh. "Kind of like it was with me and Nate."

"Stop." Gina shot her cousin a look. "You do not get to talk about Nate Desantro."

"Not even to tell you how sorry I am, or how much he and Christine belong together? I know she hates me and I don't blame her, not after what I did." Her voice wobbled, cracked. "I can't imagine what I'd do if some woman came after Robert. I don't think I'd survive." She bit her lip, blinked hard. "I can't undo the hurt I caused, but I can do my darnedest to make sure no one else causes that kind of hurt."

"You're talking about Emma.

Natalie's eyes turned bright, glittered with purpose. "Love between a couple is precious and sacred, but it's not perfect or without problems. If the couple isn't aware, they can get blindsided by women like Emma...and the old me. We swoop in and take what we want, even when it's not ours to take."

A tiny shred of sympathy swirled through Gina, but she pushed it away. "And you really think she wants Ben?"

A nod. "It's hard to get details from her. I asked about her family and she said she had a sister. Nothing about parents or what might have happened to them." A raised brow. "We both know about parents we'd rather not mention."

"Uh...yes, we do."

"But here's the thing; I don't miss the way her voice dips and goes all soft when she comments on how blue Ben's eyes are, or how many muscles he has, kind of like she thinks she has a right to them." Natalie sat up straight, lips pinched, eyes narrowed, a clear indication she took personal offense to the comment. "She's got her aim on Ben, even if it's all wrapped up in her do-gooder/angel persona."

Gina sipped air, tried to make sense of Natalie's words. "Emma could have any man she wanted. Why would she go after a married one?"

The sadness on her cousin's face said the explanation would not be a welcome one. "Because she can."

No. Gina pressed her fingers against her temples, fought the jabs that marked the beginning of a headache. "I'm the one who asked her to work with him."

"I know; she told me." Natalie reached out, placed a hand on Gina's shoulder and vowed, "I won't let her do this to you. I'm going after her, and she'll wish she'd never come to this town."

Natalie's warning burrowed into Gina's brain and refused to leave. If her cousin had come to her pre-injury with tales of a woman's interest in Ben, Gina would have shrugged and said *So, what else is new?* Cynthia Carlisle, heir to a car dynasty, had been after Ben, before *and* after his marriage. The woman didn't care that he had a wife and two children, or maybe she didn't consider Gina worthy of a man like Ben Reed. Maybe she thought *she* was the only one worthy of him because she was rich, beautiful, and had no desire to associate with ordinary-looking people like Gina. That had lost her more than one man.

There'd been other women, too: young, old, married, divorced. Ben had a way about him that drew females in and made them want to latch onto that smile, those muscles, the look that said he didn't need anybody to tell him who he was or what he wanted. He'd ignored all of them, didn't even notice the flirtatious attempts, but others did. Cash had teased him about it, but he had the same type of women after him, and they achieved the same results—zero success. Six months ago, Gina would have vowed she and Ben were solid, would remain together until they drew their last breath.

Now, she didn't know if they'd be together in six months or six weeks. They hadn't slept in the same bed since the accident, hadn't touched or held each other. When was the last time they'd kissed, even a quick peck on the lips? She'd been trying so hard to keep it all together, be everything for everyone: mother and father to the children, wife, financial and emotional supporter to her husband. But had any of it mattered? She and Ben were strangers and as the days passed, they became more adversaries than partners.

Is this what happened when a marriage began to disintegrate?

Three days after her conversation with Natalie, the answer presented itself, not with yelling or accusations; those would come later. This answer snuffed the air from the room the second she stepped through the door and took in her husband's clean-shaven jaw, damp hair, and fresh T-shirt. How had he managed *that* when he wasn't supposed to shower without help? She'd wanted to put a chair in the shower, but of course, he'd refused because that would make him look too much like a man in need of help. And he couldn't give the appearance of needing assistance, now could he? No indeed, at least not to anyone who might stop by and spot the chair, though how would that happen when he'd shunned visitors? Who knew? Nothing made sense these days, especially her husband's reasoning.

And now he'd gone and showered while she was at work? Put himself *and* his family at risk with another possible fall? A slow burn spiraled through Gina, clung to her. It would do no good to let him see her concern or annoyance, since he'd just accuse her of overreacting. She straightened the magazines on the small table next to him, picked up a coffee mug and a plate with an apple core, and let the comment slip out as a casual observation. "I see the beard's gone." She'd been after him for weeks to get rid of the mountain-man look, had even offered to help him—and he'd refused.

A swirl of red crept up her husband's clean-shaven neck, settled on his cheeks. "It started to itch, so I figured it was time."

Gina nodded, clutched the mug and plate, waited for him to say more. When had the words become so difficult to speak? The silence so deafening? They'd never struggled for words, never avoided the quiet either. Hadn't Ben once said they didn't need words to communicate? That they possessed that rare ability to *know* what the other was thinking and better, to know what the other needed even before they did? Yes, the man avoiding her gaze right now had spoken those words, and if they still held true, then he knew she wasn't pleased. Gina settled her gaze on his damp hair. Yesterday, the curls had brushed his ears, and while she could allow for a shorter appearance due to the dampness... Gina inched closer. Yesterday, dark curls brushed his neck, but today, they were gone. "Did you cut your hair?"

He rifled a hand through the subject of interest, sighed. "It was time."

Right. It had been time weeks ago, and yet Ben Reed aka Mountain-Man-is-my-new-look had refused her offers to make him look like the Ben Reed the town knew, the one everybody loved and called Hollywood handsome, gorgeous, wonderful. Uh-huh. She'd wanted to tell them to come for a visit, step inside and see how handsome and wonderful he was, especially the wonderful part. Self-pity and excuses only worked so long, and while Emma had gotten Ben moving and committed to rehab, his attitude was worse. For a woman like Gina, who believed equations could be solved if the right methods were employed, her husband's improved recovery and declining attitude were a big problem.

"So, you cut your own hair?" The man was very particular about his hair...

A throat clearing followed by "Emma did it."

"Emma? Emma cut your hair?"

Those blue eyes met hers, narrowed in challenge. "She did. Helped me shower, too."

More challenge in those eyes as if to say, *So what? What are you going to do about it?* Gina stared at a wisp of hair that had curled above his ear. Emma cut his hair, helped him shower? She'd been hired to help with rehabilitation, so Ben could regain his life, the life he and *Gina* had built. Emma Hale had not been hired to touch any part of Ben's body in a nontherapeutic way, even if it was the hair on his head. *And the shower*, she wanted to ask? *Did she help you undress? Offer to wash your back?* Visions of her husband's naked body invaded her brain. There'd been a time when she'd washed his back, and his front...and his—

Big sigh. "What's wrong now?"

He had the nerve to act annoyed? With her? What would he say if the roles were reversed? If a male therapist offered to cut *her* hair, wash *her* back? There'd be threats, maybe a punch or two. Gina held the mug and plate against her middle like a shield. "Wrong? I guess I'm wondering why you wouldn't let *me* help you." She paused, let her next words slide out with calculated precision. "Or why you'd let Emma." Oh, he didn't like that comment; she could tell by the way his eyes turned dark, his expression cold.

"She thought it would help make me feel better."

"Ah. I see." For a person who approached life through analysis and logic, Gina had not considered the variables, or the consequences of hiring Emma Hale.

"I know that tone." Ben's words filled with accusations, the brackets around his mouth deepening. "And don't try to deny it."

"If you recognize the tone, then you also recognize there's a reason for it."

"Meaning?"

She ignored the scowl, met it with one of her own. "Meaning if this family is important to you, if *I'm* important to you, then you better wake up and start acting like you want to be here." One scowl, this one bigger than the last, coupled with words that left no question as to their meaning. "And cut out the haircuts, the shaves, the showers, and whatever else happens in this house that isn't a therapy session."

6

Ben tossed the car magazine on the table, muttered a curse. Gina was in a mood again, but when wasn't she in a mood these days? He rubbed his jaw, trailed a hand over the smoothness of his new shave. She was crazy with her accusations. Oh, she didn't have to spit out the words to say what he knew was on her mind. Hell, he could imagine the words spewing from that mouth of hers, hear the tone, picture the look that could leave him with frostbite.

You've got a thing for Emma Hale.

You and Emma are too close.

You and Emma... You and Emma...

Emma was his *physical therapist,* period. Sure, she was nice to look at. Okay, better than nice. So what? Did the ring on his finger say he couldn't be around an attractive woman? According to the look his wife gave him a few minutes ago, that's exactly what it said. Damn it, he'd shaved, showered, *and* washed his hair because he was tired of seeing the look on Gina's face that said *I feel sorry for you* and *You need my help*. He did not need her help; he wanted her to be his wife, to think he was the king of her world...to love him.

But no, not Gina. She'd hurled accusations at him like a fastball and his reaction had been to retaliate. Was it really that big a deal if Emma helped him to the shower? It's not like she scrubbed his back or watched him strip. She'd stood outside and waited while he showered and dressed in sweat-pants and a T-shirt. And when he'd opened the door, she'd informed him full weight bearing started next week and the shower-guard-on-duty days were over, along with the crutches.

Now why hadn't Gina told him that was the plan? Why did she make it seem like he couldn't even *think* about a shower unless she was home to help? Was it an attempt to make him even more dependent on her? He was not a child, not a charity case who needed constant guidance and reminding of what he should do, shouldn't do...*had to do*...

It was damn exhausting and the fact that Gina thought some pretty face could make him risk his family, risk losing *her*, just pissed him off. *Did she think he was an idiot?* That he didn't care about her or the kids? What about the trust; where was that? Yeah, where was that? Emma Hale might be a burst of fresh air and wholesomeness with a calm sincerity about her and a gentleness that invited a person to relax, open up, and share.

But she was not Gina.

When was the last time his wife gave him a real smile, not one coated in sympathy and worry? Or treated him like a human being, not a project that needed fixing? And inti-macy? Hell no. Not that intimacy wouldn't require a bit of maneuvering and care, but it was possible.

If a man and woman loved each other, anything was possible, wasn't it?

Ben blew out a sigh, closed his eyes. He was so damn tired of it all. The bum leg, the crutches, the accusations…the disappointment in his wife's eyes when she looked at him. Another sigh, this one longer and louder than the last. His thoughts turned to Philly and the carefree days he'd known. When a person wasn't happy with his current situation, it was always easy to look at the past, remember it in a brighter light. Sure, there'd been the screwed-up years with Melissa and the I'm-a-tough-guy-and-I-am-not-sharing-my-feelings attitude, but there'd been good times, too: motorcycles, performance cars, the adrenaline rush of real police work, and the body that would not fail him.

Emma liked to hear the stories and he liked to tell them. What did it matter if he embellished a bit, took the memory a few inches farther than the truth? Her laughter and excitement boosted his ego, encouraged him to stretch the tales. When he shared his past life, he wasn't beaten up, broken, just shy of forty. For just a little while, he was strong, carefree, not a shell of the man he'd once been with a wife who treated him like a medical case.

He would have gone on with thoughts of Philly and his wife's attitude toward him if Nate Desantro hadn't barged in with a ticked-off look on his face and words to match. "What's going on with you and Emma Hale?"

Nate Desantro was a no-bullshit kind of guy who didn't waste time on polite inquiries or casual chit-chat. When the man asked questions, he expected answers, and those answers better contain the truth because the guy didn't like liars. No problem there, because Ben had nothing to hide—about anything, including Emma. "You don't want to sit down, grab a drink, talk about the wife and kids before you go for the jugular?"

The man frowned. "No. Not necessary."

"Okay, fine, but Gina's got a pitcher of iced tea in the kitchen and some fruity—"

"All I want are answers, Ben. Straight-up, no bullshit." Those dark eyes glittered. "Think you can do that?"

What the hell kind of question was that? "Did Gina send you?"

Nate's brows pinched together. "Gina? Of course not. Why would she send me when she's reverted to the old Gina, the one who wouldn't share a recipe, much less confessions about a wandering husband."

"Wandering husband?" Ben clutched the guardrails of the bed, hoisted himself up. "You mean cheating?" The guy had nerve, and messed-up body or not, if he didn't tone it down, Ben would lunge at him, even if he landed back in the hospital. "You're out of line, and you're way off base."

"Am I? Then why did your wife almost break down when Christine asked her how you were doing and then refuse to talk about it? And why did mention of Emma Hale send her to the bathroom for fifteen minutes and when she returned, her eyes were bloodshot, her nose swollen? Doesn't take a genius to realize there's trouble between you and Gina, and the new physical therapist in town's in the middle of it."

Gina had been crying? Did she think he cheated on her? How could she think that? Ben might be annoyed with his wife and he might not be happy with their marriage right now, but he would *never* betray her. Didn't she know that?

"Well?" Nate eyeballed him like he'd just as soon land a punch than have a conversation. "Why don't you enlighten me on your relationship with this woman because from what

I'm seeing and Christine's hearing, you've forgotten you're a married man with two children." He took a step closer, gripped the edge of the bedrail. "I have no problem reminding you if that's what it takes."

Was he serious? Ben scowled, spat out, "If a man isn't falling all over his wife because he has his own issues—" he pointed to his leg "—that doesn't mean he's going to hop into bed with someone else. Or that he already has."

Nate relaxed his grip on the bedrail, let out a quiet sigh. "You just remember that."

GINA WOKE to the garage door clanging open with a creak and a groan. Ben promised to get the door serviced in the spring, but he'd made a lot of promises that looked like they might not happen. She eased out of bed, made her way to the window, and peeked outside. Her husband stood just inside the garage, leaning on crutches, his coat open, hair windblown. He didn't seem to notice the cold as he stared at the monster machine that had followed him from Philly, a sign of his past life. A Harley motorcycle.

He hadn't ridden the bike since he returned to Magdalena to profess his love and ask Gina to marry him. She'd gained comfort in the knowledge that he'd vowed *not* to ride again without her blessing, but what would have given her greater comfort was a *For Sale* sign on the darn thing. That hadn't happened. Instead, Ben had cleaned out a corner of the garage, had the bike delivered to Magdalena, protected it with a fancy gray cover, and stuck it on a battery tender. *So the battery won't die*, he'd said. She'd wanted to ask him why it mattered if the battery lived or died since he wasn't going to ride it again, but she didn't because maybe he *did* plan to ride it one day...and maybe she'd rather not know about it. Last year, she'd mentioned they could use extra space in the garage and maybe it was time to reorganize. She'd never come right out and said *sell the bike*, but the cold stare told her he knew what she was hinting at, and the scowl said the bike wasn't for sale.

Gina squinted into the night, fixed her gaze on the brightness of the garage, and watched as Ben moved toward the bike, leaned on one crutch, and worked the cover off. He ran a hand along the leather seat, slow and soft, like a caress, his fingers stilling, then continuing on. Was he remembering his other life, the one filled with daring police work, motorcycle rides, and the exhilaration of near misses?

No one to hold him back, no cozy home, no questions or comments about what he should or shouldn't do. *Was he wishing he were back in that life?*

She stayed by the window as he dragged a folding chair toward the bike and maneuvered his long body into it, placing the crutches at his side. The man in the garage was brooding, distant, untouchable. *Where was her husband and would he ever return?*

Fear that he would not return solidified six days later when she arrived home after a Saturday afternoon grocery trip. Cash had agreed to hang out at the house and watch the kids with Ben—because her husband could not perform child duty on his own—and Gina had agreed. Ben needed male companionship and who better than the best friend and ex-partner who'd been shot up and suffered his own physical and emotional injuries? She had just turned onto their street when she heard the thrum of an engine that could only belong to one sort of vehicle: a motorcycle. And since the

Reeds were the only family who housed a motorcycle in their garage, albeit one that remained on a battery tender, the sound either came from Ben's bike or the neighborhood had a visitor. Gina would have opted for the second choice if Cash weren't sitting on the bike in question, and Ben weren't two feet away with the kind of smile on his face she hadn't seen in months.

Maybe she'd have let the foolishness go and classified it as men's bonding if she hadn't spotted the tiny hands wrapped around Cash's waist. *Alex!* Gina zoomed up the driveway, threw the car in park, and jumped out. "What are you doing?" She rushed toward them, fists clenched, anger spewing. "Get him off that bike! Now!"

Cash shut it down, his face a burst of red. "I'm sorry, Gina. We didn't mean to scare you." He clutched Alex's small hands with one of his own. "I wouldn't let anything happen to him."

She ignored his apology, turned to Ben. "Are you trying to plant the seed in our son's brain so he'll want one of these the second he's old enough?" The slash of lips and clenched jaw told her he was not happy with her outburst. Too bad. She had a lot to say and she'd kept it in too long.

"You're overreacting, Gina. There's no harm letting him sit on the bike."

"Oh? You mean the bike you promised you wouldn't ride? The one you insisted you had to keep charged so the battery wouldn't die? Why did it matter if the battery died if you never planned to ride it again?" She jabbed a finger at the black motorcycle. "Who do you think you were fooling?" More anger spilled in waves of frustration and accusation. "Me or yourself?"

He sighed his disgust. "You don't know what you're

talking about because you're too damn busy controlling situations that can't be controlled."

"Dad! Swear word," Alex said, peeking at his father from behind Cash's shoulder.

Ben dragged a hand over his face, gentled his voice, "Sorry, Alex." He moved toward the bike, grabbed Alex, and eased him from the back of the bike. "Here you go," he said, setting him on the ground. "Now run inside and finish your peanut butter and jelly sandwich. Two squares won't build muscle."

Their son nodded, darted a glance at Gina. "I asked Dad and Uncle Cash to sit on the bike, Mom." His bottom lip quivered. "It wasn't Dad's fault."

"Alex, this is adult business. Your father and I will discuss what happened." Pause. "And what *should* have happened."

"But—"

"Listen to your mother," Ben said, his voice tight. "Rules are rules in our house, and we can't forget them or your mother will remind us."

Cash cleared his throat. "How about I put the bike away and help get the groceries in the house before I take off?"

Gina nodded. "Thank you." No doubt he'd tell Tess about the fireworks he'd witnessed in the Reeds' driveway, and Tess would tell Christine who would tell Bree... They were all worried about her and she appreciated it, but this was her problem—whatever *this* was. She shot a glance at Ben who ignored her and headed toward the house.

He didn't talk to her again until she'd put away the groceries and was chopping carrots and red peppers for the hummus she'd made yesterday. Ava would wake from her nap soon and then it would be dinnertime, and baths... Before the accident, she could count on Ben to help with diapers, meals, story time, anything she wanted, but now it all depended on his mood of the moment. Well, she was tired of it and today he'd pushed her too far.

Ben stood in the doorway of the kitchen, blue gaze narrowed, lips pinched. She knew that look, knew what it meant, too. The man was sparring for a fight. Gina tossed a carrot stick onto a plate, continued slicing, and waited. She made it through a whole carrot before Ben spoke.

"So, what was that all about? Are you pissed at me or Cash, or are you just pissed at the whole world because Gina Reed can't control the entire population with her rules and her demands?"

Gina glanced up, set the knife aside. "It was about going back on a promise you made me."

The left side of his jaw twitched. "I did not break any promise to you."

She raised a brow, tried to remain calm. "I don't ask a lot, but that motorcycle was off limits, and the fact that you'd let our son on it bothers me as much as it confuses me. What's it going to be next? Wait until I'm gone and then take a spin with him around the block, and when I find out, then what? You'll get mad or change the terms of our agreement so you can do whatever you want?" Her breath fell out faster, harder. "Is that how this is going to be?"

Ben made his way into the kitchen and braced himself against the counter. "No, it's not. I didn't think it was a big deal to let Alex sit on the back of the bike."

"The bigger question is why you and Cash were out there." The deep red snaking up his neck said she wouldn't like the answer. "Of course. You wanted to hear the sound of it, maybe think about what it was like to ride, maybe even wish you were on that bike, hundreds of miles away from all of this." His silence tore at her soul, told her what she'd surmised those nights when she'd watched from the bedroom window as he sat in the garage staring at that blasted bike. He missed that life, wished he had it back.

"Sure, I miss it; only an idiot wouldn't." He looked away, said in a quiet voice, "But I made a promise and I won't break it."

"But you want to, don't you?" Gina clutched the edge of the counter, sipped in tiny breaths. "I've been watching you at night, sitting in the garage, mooning over that damn motorcycle—"

"You're spying on me?" Anger and disbelief flashed across his face. "Why would you do that?" And then, "Is that what this marriage has been reduced to—spying?"

She would not let him play the outraged victim, not after he'd rejected everything she'd tried to give him: her help, her guidance, her love. Gina let out a cold laugh. "This marriage has been reduced by a lot more than spying. In fact, I don't even recognize it, or you, anymore." He flinched, recovered so fast she almost thought she'd imagined the reaction, but the starkness on his face said her comments had affected him, even if he didn't want her to see.

7

Since the blowout in the garage the other day, Cash made a point to check in on Ben every day. Sure, he made it look like a random visit that included deliveries: homemade pizza with jalapeños and pepperoni, a current issue of *Muscle Car Review* magazine, a batch of chili, a six-pack of dark ale. The gifts were a nice lead-in to what his buddy was really doing here: checking up on him. As if Ben couldn't see that one ten miles away. He was a cop, and he sniffed out Cash's reasons for the visits partway through the first one, but after visit number four in as many days, Ben was done with the pretense.

He had a question for Cash that had been rolling around in his head since the garage incident and he'd debated asking, but now he figured, why not? Ben sat up straight in the recliner he and Gina used to cozy up on and pushed out the words. "Do you ever miss Philly?"

Dead silence followed by the darkest frown Ben had seen in a long time. "Miss Philly?"

He could tell by the tone in Cash's voice that he knew

exactly what Ben meant: the adrenaline rush, the chase, the constant pulse of excitement. There was nothing like it, especially when you weren't afraid of anything, probably because you had nothing to lose. "Right, Philly."

Not a second's hesitation as Cash shook his head. "Nope. Not a bit."

Ben couldn't let it go at that. They'd shared too much, and Cash had been too good at his job to not miss it a little bit. "You were the best damn marksman the force had ever seen. You don't miss being the best just a little bit?" Ben had to ask because there was a tiny piece of him that *did* miss being the best at something that drew attention, awe, praise.

Cash shrugged. "I developed a skill and I was good at it, but with that skill came an expectation and a lot of risk. You can't have one without the other. I'd never want to go back to that life, the not knowing what waited on the other side of the door, or if I'd make it home. All I had back then was the job, but I've got a wife and kids now." His gaze narrowed on Ben, pierced the first and second layers behind the conversation, and the spark in those eyes said he saw more than he should have—and didn't like what he saw. "I'd never take that risk again."

"You don't think there's a way to have a piece of it?" Some days he wanted to feel invincible again, like nothing could touch him—like he wasn't looking at forty with a wife and kids, a mortgage, a busted leg...

"Doesn't work that way. You're either all in or you're all out. I'm a dad now. I read about magical tree houses with bunnies to one kid and I'm teaching the other how to catch and clean a fish. I'm happy and it's taken a long time to get here. I don't need to be a badass to feel like I'm worth something." He paused, said in a quiet voice. "You shouldn't either."

"I know that... Of course, I know that. I'm not saying I want to be the first through the door, but maybe I don't want to be the last in anything either." The look Cash gave him said he didn't like that answer.

"What's this really about?"

Ben rubbed his jaw, looked away. "It's about not wanting to miss out before it's too late...sometimes wondering if it's already too late." There. He'd said it.

"Too late for what?"

Ben didn't miss the shreds of disgust and annoyance smothered in his friend's words. Okay, maybe the guy *didn't* get it. Maybe he really did like to read fairy tales and go fishing. Or maybe it was Ben who didn't get it; maybe he was just an ungrateful jerk who wanted more than life as an old, busted up has-been.

"This is about that damn woman, isn't it?" Anger flashed across Cash's face. "Emma Hale's filling your head with bullshit, making you forget you have a wife, kids, responsibilities. She's spinning a tale about going after life, taking a big bite out of it, and doing any damn thing you want. Whenever you want. Don't have to answer to anybody. *That's* fairy tale bullshit and if you listen to her you're going to lose the best thing that ever happened to you."

"This isn't about Emma or trying to be thirty again." But even as he said the words he knew they weren't true. He *wanted* to feel needed, looked up to, important, and his wife didn't think of him that way, not anymore. He'd become an obligation and a nuisance. Hadn't she told him if he couldn't put on a decent face in front of the kids then maybe he shouldn't be here? Well, maybe he *shouldn't* be here. Not now, not until he got his head straight.

"Ben, listen to me." Cash stood, crossed his arms over his chest. "I don't know if it's that woman or a midlife crisis or too many hours alone, but you do not want to step outside the boundaries, because Gina will toss your ass out so fast you won't even realize what's happened until it's too late."

"Do I not have a say in anything anymore, even my own life?" He dragged both hands over his face, blew out a long sigh. He was so damn tired of it all. "Does Gina get to tell me how it's going to be? Maybe she'll organize *me* in one of her lists." He let out a harsh laugh, considered the possibility that his wife had a notebook with his name in it. "Why don't you look around and see if you can find a notebook with my name on it. Bet you will. *Ben Reed—Long-term Project.*"

"Now you're just being a jerk."

"Maybe I am a jerk."

"Maybe you are," Cash shot back. "You can sit here and feel sorry for yourself, which is such a bunch of BS, even I'm getting tired of the pity party, and I'm your friend. I've got a few questions for you. Why are you still sleeping in a hospital bed in the middle of your living room when you should be sleeping with your wife? And stop with the evil-eye because unless Gina's crawling into that damn contraption—" he pointed to the metal hospital bed "—you're not sleeping together."

"It's too difficult to climb the stairs." Maybe that would have been true weeks ago, but it wasn't true now, and Cash knew it.

"*That's* your story? You really are a jerk. And a baby." Cash blew out his disgust. "I remember those days, lying in bed like the whole world was a giant cesspool and I was right in the middle of it. Gina used to come to my aunt's and give me therapy. That woman called me out five minutes after she walked in the door, told me I was wasting my aunt's money because I should be further along with my therapy and would be if I stopped self-medicating." He nodded, his lips twitching. "She's a tough one, but loyal. Determined. Strong."

"Yup, that's Gina. Self-sufficient, too. Don't forget that one."

Another sigh, this one louder and more annoyed than the last. "She's your wife and the best thing that ever happened to your sorry ass. You better get this not sleeping together crap fixed fast. That is not good."

"Hey, enough." Gina would not be happy if she knew Cash was pondering their sex life. Or lack of it.

"Sure. Right. But there're only two reasons you're not back in your wife's bed. It's kind of like the car that hasn't been on the road for a while and now you're taking it on a trip. What do you worry about?"

Was he really going to go there? *Damn him.* Ben's jaw twitched. "No idea."

That made him laugh. "Sorry, but I'm not buying that one. We've both been around enough cars in our day to know we'd be thinking about—" he eyed him a second too long "—performance."

Ben was not touching that comment. Nope, not doing it. Why would he admit to worrying about a damn performance issue when he couldn't even admit it to himself? Would he disappoint his wife? Would he be able to maneuver around her body? Would he be able to—

"Yup, I see you're thinking about that one."

"Or maybe you just planted it in my head so I *would* think about it. Damn, but you are such a jerk." No guy wanted to consider a malfunction in that area, not even the ones who'd never come close to having an issue—like Ben. But once it crept into a guy's head, it could set up camp and then what? *Yeah, then what?* Ben tried to snuff out the thought with his next question. "So, what's the other reason? You said there were two?" Now the guy was going to start on his reduced muscle mass, puny core strength, dwindling quads. But when Cash spoke, it wasn't that at all.

"You're getting it somewhere else."

Sex, that's what he meant. "Say that again and bum leg or not, I'll lunge out of this chair and we'll go at it."

"Right. Because you're all about honor and taking care of those you love." Cash fisted his hands on his hips, stared Ben down. "I am not going to sit back and watch you destroy the best thing that ever happened to you without shoving your face in it. Maybe you really can't see that Miss-I'm-out-to-heal-the-world is out to steal Ben Reed from his family, but you'd better open your eyes and do it fast before you step on a landmine."

"Meaning?" Why couldn't people believe that goodwill and kindness for the sake of helping others still existed? Why did they always have to think an ulterior motive smothered in self-interest was involved?

Cash stepped toward him, his mouth a slash of anger. "Meaning if you don't straighten up, dump the therapist, and make things right with your wife, your life is going to explode." More anger spilled from that mouth, targeting Ben with the firearm precision that had earned awe and respect from fellow officers. "And then you'll see what real pain is like." He went for the kill shot. "You'll lose Gina and learn the meaning of all alone."

NATALIE SERVETTI TRIMBLE sat in Mimi's kitchen, hands folded in her lap, dark hair pulled back in a ponytail. She was a beautiful woman, and the fact that she no longer hid behind layers of eyeliner or too tight clothing made her even more beautiful. No more tennis-ball-sized hoops in her ears, no necklaces dipping beneath a plunging neckline, nothing but tiny diamond studs and a diamond ring—testaments to love, second chances, and new beginnings. Pop thought Natalie and her husband were a good match and Mimi agreed. She liked Richard Trimble, but then the quiet types with the calm demeanor and steady personality reminded Mimi of Roger, her late husband. Pop believed Richard and their new baby made Natalie a different person, but Mimi knew it was more than that.

Natalie *wanted* to be different, wanted to be done with the life she'd led and the lies she'd told. Most of the town didn't quite believe her, but Mimi did, maybe because she'd seen the truth in the girl's eyes or maybe because she'd known enough people who'd reformed. Life was about second chances, hope, and the belief that you could start over. Mimi had seen it with friends and loved ones, even had that chance herself. Since her reunion with her daughter, Jennifer, Mimi believed miracles *could* happen, and Natalie Servetti Trimble's transformation was indeed a true miracle.

The girl sat across from her, a cup of tea and a plate containing two chocolate chip cookies sitting untouched. The look on Natalie's face told the tale of sadness and remorse. A person should not suffer when she wanted to do right and was sorry for her transgressions. Mimi would make the town see that Natalie deserved a second chance.

"Have your tea and a chocolate chip cookie. There's no need to be nervous in front of me." She eased the cookies closer to Natalie, offered a gentle smile. "I'm hungry for one and it's not polite to eat in front of company."

The young woman worked up a smile, lifted a cookie from the plate. "Thank you, Mrs. Pendergrass, for taking the time to see me. I've given you no reason to listen to anything I have to say, but I do appreciate it."

"It's Mimi, dear, just Mimi. And I appreciate the fact that you want to help Ben. Anything you can tell me that will get him and Gina over this rough spot is worth listening to, don't you think?"

Natalie nodded, her dark head shining under the kitchen light. Was that shine natural or had the girl learned a few tricks to enhance the look? Mimi sure would like to know the secret and maybe one day she'd ask Natalie, or maybe she'd visit her at Natalie's Salon & Spa. People liked it, at least the ones like Tess Casherdon and Bree Kinkaid Brandon who hadn't been afraid of attaching a smell to their name by visiting Natalie's new salon. They said the girl had talent and it would just take time and a willingness to forgive for the rest of the town to realize that.

"So—" Mimi sipped her tea, considered her information-gathering strategy, settled on straight-up asking "—what do you know that could help Gina and Ben get through what looks like a mess waiting to happen?"

"Emma Hale isn't as squeaky clean as people think she is." Pink slithered along Natalie's neck to her chin, burst onto her cheeks like fireworks. "I'm the last person who should be bad-mouthing someone, but I can't watch Gina get hurt again." Pause, a quiver of her bottom lip that spilled regret.

"She's been through so much, most of it caused by her own relatives, including me."

Mimi patted the girl's hand, tried to head off the tears that looked like they were about to spill any second. "I know, dear, I know. Mistakes of the past are best kept in the past. All we can do now is move on and learn from them." Another pat, a smile and a soft "I do believe you've learned from the past, Natalie."

"I have." Her voice wobbled. "I truly have."

"I'd like to help Ben and Gina get back to where they were before the accident, so whatever you can tell me will help."

"Emma came to the salon a week or so after she moved here, said she wanted to find a place she could trust to take care of her nails and such. She asked me a bunch of questions, commented on how clear my skin was, how nice my nails looked, asked about technique, inspected my tools, and then she booked a series of appointments with me: facials, mani-pedicures, waxing."

Perhaps the new physical therapist was a bit overzealous in regard to hiring out personal care, but how was that relevant to Ben and Gina? Mimi opened her mouth to ask that very question when Natalie answered it.

"You can find out an awful lot about a person when you're working a pumice stone on their foot calluses or wrapping their face in a towel. These gestures are intimate and encourage sharing." She shrugged, nibbled her bottom lip. "The separateness falls away and the sharing starts. Happens every time. The key is to listen and not feel compelled to offer answers. That's what happened with Emma." Her dark brows pinched together. "I don't gossip, but this is important. I tried to tell Gina about my suspicions, but I don't think she wanted to believe it, or maybe she just didn't want to hear anything that came from me." She swiped a cheek, sniffed. "Maybe I should have gone straight to Nate and talked to him, but I didn't think that was a good idea."

No, it was not. A person didn't tell the man whose marriage she almost tore apart that she had *anything* to say to him. "I think that was wise."

"But I thought maybe you could talk to him because Nate Desantro holds a lot of sway in this town. Gina might listen to him, or she might listen to Christine." Natalie clasped her hands in her lap, sucked in a breath, and let the story spill. "Emma told me when she first started coming in that she almost fell for one of her patients in Philly, but a few days ago, the truth spilled out. She was head-over-heels for the guy, planned on a future with him. The guy got hit by a car while jogging: broke his leg, his pelvis, dislocated his shoulder. It was months of therapy and they got close. Too close. She said their relationship was so much deeper than physical. Emma called it a spiritual journey to peace and fulfillment. Guess the guy sold her a story, said she was the reason for his recovery and if not for her, he would have given up." Her eyes turned bright, glittered with tears. "Of course, he said the wife didn't care about him, that they'd been heading for a divorce before the accident, but he had to go slow because of the two kids. It was all a line and she believed it."

"Dear me." Mimi shook her head, considered the pain of learning those lies. "What happened when she discovered the truth?"

Natalie shrugged. "I don't know; Emma said it wasn't meant to be, but something in her tone made me think she didn't just pack up and leave without a fight."

"This doesn't sound like the Emma the town's been

spouting on and on about as a miracle worker and gentle soul for the sick and needy." Mimi set her cup on the table with a thud. "This one sounds like she doesn't understand or respect boundaries, professional or personal."

"That's what I'm worried about. She's been talking about Ben and how wonderful he is, like there's no Gina. It's creepy. I think we should find out what really happened in Philly, and how she ended up here. She says it was destiny, that she tossed a penny on an open map and chose the closest small town." Natalie picked up a cookie, studied it. "I'm not sure I believe that."

Mimi wasn't sure she believed it either. The tale made an interesting story, but it sure had the ring of fiction to it. She rubbed her jaw, tried to recall conversations she and the woman had when she'd visited Magdalena for an interview with the hospital. But like the rest of the town, Mimi had been pulled in by the fresh-faced pledge to *help others and make a difference in a small-town setting* that she hadn't considered an ulterior motive. Why wouldn't people in this town believe Emma? "Well, I didn't hear about the penny story, but I did hear, firsthand, how she wanted to help our town. I must say, she made a convincing presentation, so much so that I didn't once think it was contrived."

"I know." Natalie's voice rose two decibels, spilled with worry and dread. "She's very good at making people believe what she wants them to, whether it's true or not. What if she manipulates Ben somehow and destroys his marriage?" Another sniff, a double blink that caught fresh tears. "He would never cheat on Gina, but Emma could lie about it and say he did or try to push Gina out. I've seen it all before...I've done it all before..."

The tears did fall this time, big, fat ones sliding down her cheeks. Mimi reached over and squeezed Natalie's hand. "It's okay, dear. Those days are long past. You aren't that person any longer. You must stop punishing yourself for what can't be changed."

A nod, more tears. "I hurt so many people and I am so sorry."

"I know, but all you can do now is exactly what you're doing." Pause, another squeeze of her hand and a gentle "I'm proud of you, Natalie. I truly am." Mimi swiped at a tear. This woman wanted to do right, and she deserved the chance.

"We have to find out her secrets," Natalie said. "She's got them. I can tell by the faraway sound of her voice and how she looks away when she doesn't want to answer a question. And what about the angel-touch and nobody-like-her reviews we've all heard about? They flitted through town the second she landed here. I think *she* started the stories and I bet they aren't even all true."

"I've wondered about the glowing reviews attached to her achievements. There usually aren't so many and they aren't so extraordinary." Even Grant Richot, the pediatric neurosurgeon who'd once operated on children's brains, did not garner such attention when he came to town. True, he'd preferred to maintain a low profile, but still...children's brains? But word had it Emma Hale had not been shy about offering up her successes or her abilities to her patients or anyone willing to listen.

The whole town had been so caught up in the glitter of those accolades they'd not considered the possibility that they might not be true. Or if they were true, there was more to the story, one that involved falling in love with patients, a definite no-no in the medical world. "Well, this is certainly getting interesting."

"Emma might make a play for Ben," Natalie said, her voice filled with emotion. "But he'd never cheat on Gina. No way. Ben loves her. They belong together."

"Seduction isn't the only way to cause problems in a marriage. If a third party starts rumors, doubt gets in the way of seeing the truth."

"We've got to stop her." Natalie's face lit up with determination. "I will not let her destroy Ben and Gina's marriage, so tell me what to do and I'll do it."

8

Thirteen weeks after the accident

Gina stared at her husband, tried to process what he'd just said. "You want to go to Philly? Why?"

His gaze darted to the carpet, shifted to the base of the television stand, anywhere so he didn't have to look at her, admit straight-up what was really going on. It was easier to massage a truth if you didn't have to look a person in the eye —especially if that person was your wife. These past several weeks her husband had become an avoider of details, emotions, and the truth.

"In case it's not obvious, I'm stumbling around with a lot of questions right now. Philly might clear my head." He rubbed his jaw and when he spoke this time, he *did* look at her, his expression a shadow of the old Ben. "I'm just asking you to be patient."

Patient? Had she not been patient while he recovered from his injury, pushed her away and told her he didn't *need* her, didn't *want* her help? That he preferred Emma Hale's touch? Maybe he hadn't come out and said that, but the implications were there. And had that touch been pure therapy or had it grown more intimate? Was *that* why he hadn't tried to touch her since the accident? Oh, she had a lot to say about patience, but she bit the inside of her cheek so she didn't blurt it all out, because once she started with words like *how dare you* and *damn you*, or *what gives you the right*, she might not stop until she kicked him out of the house.

And then what?

She sipped air, forced her brain to slow down and remain calm. "How will you get there? Driving around town isn't the same as driving to Philly."

"It's four hours, plus my driving leg is fine." He cleared his throat, added, "The doctor gave me the okay."

"He did? You called him?" Ben never called doctors' offices, that was Gina's job, had been since they said "I do." Apparently, not anymore.

He nodded. "He said to listen to my body and take breaks."

"I see." She didn't see anything other than the widening fracture in their marriage. "How long will you be gone?"

That handsome face pinched with what could only be called guilt, a sure sign the words he spoke were not one hundred percent true or accurate. "Four days, maybe six. Rudy's not ready for me to come back to work yet, so that shouldn't be a problem. And I know Tess has the kids covered, so..."

Ben's words squeezed her heart. This was what happened when you loved someone too much; this was what happened when they didn't love you back. There was no need to ask if the trip would be a solo one; she already knew the answer.

The woman Gina hired to give her husband back his life would accompany him. They would relive memories of a city they'd both shared, and Gina, the children, and the life Ben had in Magdalena would not be part of that. He would discard them and find a new life, an exciting one with the woman who told him he was perfect, invincible, the light of the world—even if it weren't true. *She* would expect nothing from him and he, in his desire to be young and carefree again would accept it as true and honest love.

He dragged a hand over his face, let out a long, slow sigh. "I know I'm asking a lot, but I need this, Gina."

Of course, he did; didn't all men on the verge of a midlife crisis need to get away, find situations and people who wouldn't question their actions? She opened her mouth to tell him this, say *Who do you think you're fooling, Ben Reed? I've slept beside you, birthed your babies, and I am not an idiot or a fool. I know exactly what you're doing and why, even if you don't or can't admit it.* But that would be too much truth right now, so she cleared her throat and said instead, "If it's what you need to do, then do it."

He eyed her as if trying to determine the sincerity of her words, settled on "Thanks." And then, in a softer voice reminiscent of the man she'd married, "Thanks for understanding."

Understanding? Oh, she understood all right, but not the way he thought. A woman could only take so much before she exploded, and those last words proved Gina's undoing. She balled her hands into fists to keep from lunging at him as the truth flew out. "Understanding? I don't understand anything. Not why you're doing this, or how we ended up so far apart, or when it will stop... Even *if* it will stop. But I really don't have a choice, do I? I can accept what you're offering, or I can reject it and you're still going to do exactly what you want, just like you've been doing since the accident." Anger and truth blended, spewed from her lips. "So go. Go and do what you need to do: find yourself, find your life, find your purpose. I hope you realize that every minute you're gone, every day the separation between us widens, will be that much more difficult to get back to the way we were." One more truth slipped out. "And I'm starting to think that's your plan."

∼

THERE COMES a time in a man's life when he's got to own up to his issues and do something about them, and for Ben, the key was a trip to Philly. Gina didn't agree, but then she hadn't agreed with much of anything he'd said these past few months, and with good reason. He'd been a beast: unpleasant, ornery, sullen. That's what happened when an accident snuffed out the perfect life you had, stole your body's ability to perform, cast doubt on the future. Hell, you didn't even know if you *had* a future, let alone what it might look like. Would your body recover so you could return to police work that was about more than desk duty? Would you be able to run, climb ladders again, make love to your wife without the nagging fear that something would give out?

Too many hours considering all the potential disasters can leave a man with uncertainties that morph into fears and the dread he'll be a quarter of the man he used to be.

And then what? *Then the hell what?* He'd woken up more than once in a cold sweat as dreams of inadequacies plagued him. Was this it? If he couldn't achieve full recovery, what would that look like? How would he handle it? No sense pretending forty wasn't staring him down. Were the best years behind him or was this accident a wake-up call to grab onto the years he had left, dive into them? But then what? He'd gain his strength back and act like he was thirty again?

Did he really *want* to be thirty again with all the BS that went with it? Thirty hadn't been a particularly stellar age for him, but he didn't like to admit that. No, the best age for him had been when he met Gina and every year after that—even thirty-nine looking at forty. But Emma had gone on and on about diving into life, and in his self-pity, he'd bought into the hype. It didn't matter that he had no idea what "diving into life" meant, or that if he were going to dive anywhere, he wanted his wife beside him. Well forget that last one because Gina wasn't interested in going *anywhere* with him.

Could he blame her? He just needed her to hang in there a little longer until he got his head straight. Philly would do that, and then he'd have a plan. Gina liked plans. Life could be good again. Maybe. But not until he figured out a few things...

An hour after arriving in Philly, Ben knew it was not the same place he'd left four years ago. He'd only been back once, to meet with a real estate agent and pack up a few things from the condo: four boxes, most of them clothes, a few pictures, two books, and a frying pan he favored. What did that say about him and the life he'd led? Some might consider him a minimalist who didn't need *things* to achieve happiness. Others might say the lack of important belongings signaled a detached existence, numbness to his surroundings, and a refusal to engage in life. He didn't believe in the mumbo-jumbo of philosophers, but he'd go with the second, because the house he and Gina shared held a lot of memories and belongings he *couldn't* leave behind.

Everything had a meaning, from Alex and Ava's birth announcements sitting on the mantel, framed and decorated with Gina's pressed flowers, to the stress-reducing pillow she bought him to support his neck when he watched TV.

And what about the coffee mug Alex gave him last Father's Day with the boy's smiling face plastered on it? Couldn't give that one up either. Or the blue ribbon Lily Desantro handed him last year when he won the "Pounds for Pets" weightlifting competition. Of course, there were the intangible attachments as well, and those would be even harder, if not impossible, to leave: Gina's smile when he told her she was his world, Alex's laughter when his sister made cooing sounds, Ava's chubby fingers gripping his. Simple, heart-pinging, irreplaceable.

Ben wanted to be the man he'd been, but how could he do that with so many doubts clouding his head? Philly represented a time when his body had been strong, his attitude invincible. Since the accident he'd grown weak and uncertain, filled with doubt and fear that he couldn't be the man he needed to be, the one who would protect his family. But that wasn't all he'd left in Philly, and he might as well be honest about it; he'd left his freedom there and a life that did not require permission *or* acceptance from anyone. Maybe that's why his first marriage had tanked. Okay, there was a whole trust issue buried in there and *that's* why his first marriage had tanked. He trusted Gina more than he'd ever trusted anyone, and he wanted to be the man she wanted, but did she have to expect so damn much from him?

What about what *he* wanted? What about the Harley sitting in the garage, covered and hooked up to a battery tender? He hadn't ridden since he left Philly and while Gina didn't come out and say she wanted him to sell the bike, he'd seen the look on her face when he mentioned the Harley. Fear. Worry. Distrust that he might still want to get on the thing and ride when he had a family to think about. Guilt and the desire to please her had made him transport the bike to Magdalena by truck rather than ride it there. All that worry something was going to happen to him if he got on the bike again, and it had been a friggin' trip to the attic that had taken him out.

This visit to Philly would help him come to terms with his old life and the choices he'd made, the good and the bad, so he could move forward. His grandmother used to say people had a way of taking a paintbrush to the past and covering up the parts they wanted to change with bold colors, so you couldn't see the disappointments and the mistakes. Pop Benito said you couldn't go back to a time and place no matter how much you wanted to because you aren't that same person anymore.

His grandmother and Pop Benito were both right. Ben had spent the first afternoon with his buddies on the police force, checked out the city, drank beer and reminisced about the old days. But the memories living in his head were a lot better than reality and it didn't take a genius to see that. Philly might hold the constant motion of the city life Ben had once loved, with enough great food to keep him occupied for weeks, but it wasn't home. Magdalena was home. His chest squeezed. *Gina was his home.* They belonged together, but he needed this time to figure out why he'd grown so distant with her. What did he really want from life that he couldn't do now? Ride his motorcycle along Route 66? Buy another sports car and open it up on a straight stretch of road? *What did he really want?*

Hell if he knew and maybe it was the not knowing that

drove him crazy, or maybe what he really wanted was *the choice* to do it. Yeah, maybe that was it, but as he finished his scotch with one of his old buddies, he realized that wasn't it at all and it took a washed-up cop to make him see the truth. Archer Hannah had just finished his third whiskey. Or was it his fourth? How many had the guy pounded down before Ben got to the dingy bar that used to be their hangout? Hard to tell but the bleary eyes and the nostalgia dripping from the guy's mouth said it was already one too many.

"Why are you really back here, Ben? Did you miss us?" A pause followed by a chuckle. "Miss the life? Maybe wanted to give it another go?"

Ben shrugged, slid him a smile. "Naw, just needed a little break and I was curious to see what you guys were up to these days."

"Huh. You've been gone over four years, snuggled up in that dot-on-the-map town, a lifetime away from here. Can't say I blame you." He let out a loud sigh, stared into his empty glass. "We had our time, didn't we? Me, you, Cash..." A frown pulled at his thin lips, spread across his face. "Everything's pretty much gone to shit since you left. I'm on my third marriage and this one's not looking so good either. I never see my kids...get accused of drinking too much. What kind of bullshit is that? Drinking too much. What's too much as long as you can handle it, right?"

Ben stared at his old friend, didn't answer.

Archer didn't seem to notice, but plowed on. "Police work's tough. We're not easy people to understand. I mean, you walk out the door in the morning and you never know what's gonna face you. Is it a gun, a drunk-and-disorderly that might blow your face off, a domestic dispute, drugs? Used to be we had a chance. Hell, not anymore. Who can blame us if we need a little help getting through the night, keeping the voices quiet to boost us through the next day?" He stared at Ben, nudged his arm. "Know what I mean?"

"Uh, sure."

Archer shook his head. "You and Cash are the smart ones; we all said you were. Sure, we ragged on you about quitting and getting all soft on us, but we were just jealous because we wanted to be the ones getting away." Another shake of his head. "Didn't have the guts to do it. You did, though. You and Cash sure got out. Maybe a bullet chased him out of town and maybe your ex-wife's Assistant DA asshole forced you away, but you're the lucky ones." He rubbed a stubbled jaw, his words thick, clogged with emotion. "You got a second chance and you took it."

More jaw rubbing, followed by a long sigh. "I had a chance to start over and what do you think I did?" He let out a laugh filled with sadness and too much remorse. "I screwed up. Yup, that's me, screw-up of the year. I had a good woman, but she was too good for me. I cheated on her and do you know why? Because she was strong and independent and didn't need me for her oxygen. She needed me to be a *partner*, but I needed an ego booster. So, you know what I did?" He slid Ben a look, his bloodshot eyes filled with tears.

"No." Ben did not want to hear his friend's sad story.

"I slept with the first young thing who looked my way. I didn't care about her, and she sure as hell didn't care about me, but it didn't matter because it was all about making me feel young again—invincible, needed, a hero. When the fun was over, so was my marriage. The second marriage was a repeat, and by the third, I was an old has-been with too many regrets and kids who didn't want to see me."

Archer Hannah was in his late forties, but he sounded

years older, looked it, too. Ben tried to think of something to say, grabbed the first thought that hit him. "I always liked Louise." He remembered when Archer's first wife used to send in banana-nut muffins and cinnamon coffee cakes, said it was her way of saying *thank you* for keeping her husband safe. Six months before Ben left the force, the muffins and cakes stopped, and he'd never thought to ask why. What kind of friend didn't know his buddy was getting a divorce? The self-absorbed kind who couldn't get out of his own way...

"I've never loved a woman like I loved Louise, and I don't think I ever will again, but it's too damn late. She's married to some doctor now, a cardiologist, and I've got nothing but regret." He squinted at Ben, said in a powerful voice, "Don't get sucked in by regret, Ben. Life's what you make it, not what you read about in the newspapers. It's about the here and now and making time count with somebody you really care about, not some young skirt who tells you what you want to hear instead of what you need to hear."

Why was he staring as though he thought Ben were caught between a good choice and a bad one? "Thanks for the advice, Archer. Appreciate it."

The man nodded, pushed his glass toward the bartender for another refill. "You got it, Ben. I always liked you. Go back to your wife and kids, bury the past, and don't screw up like I did. Once you do the deed, there's no going back, and then you have to keep pushing the drinks to get through the day. Don't do that."

His old friend's words stayed with him as Ben sat in his hotel room, sipping scotch and thinking about his life. How had he gotten so off course? Since the accident, he'd spent so much time running from fear that he'd ignored the only truth that mattered: he loved his life with his family. He didn't want to give that up or lose it or trade it, but he hated the uncertainty that plagued him, the questions about his own mortality. Thirty-nine would soon be forty, forty would be fifty, fifty would be sixty, sixty-five...

Then what? When he lay in bed with a body that would not cooperate, he thought of all the reasons to run and grasp onto a few minutes of living before his body gave out and he lost everything. What he hadn't realized was that if he lost Gina and the kids, then he may as well dive in the grave right now because *they* were his everything.

That truth hit him hard and fast, made him open his mouth and suck in air. Gina and the kids *were* his life and they would not make him feel old or worthless. They would make him feel needed, wanted, loved, no matter what, and it had taken a trip to Philly and the pitiful words of a friend with too many regrets to make him see that.

9

When Gina contacted Emma to tell her they needed to talk, the woman attempted to side-step a meeting with *I'm on my way out of town, can't this wait?*

No, it couldn't wait. In fact, what she had to say was long overdue, as in weeks. She'd spent most of last night imagining Emma and Ben on their way to Philly—together. But the woman was still in Magdalena, though according to her comment, not for long. Was she on her way to meet Ben? Was she planning to help him sort out his issues?

When Gina opened the door a short while later, Emma breezed in, tossed a smile and a "hello" her way, and headed for the living room, where she cozied up in Ben's recliner. "You wanted to talk?" She unzipped her jacket, slipped it off. "I don't have much time, but you said it was important. Are the kids okay?"

This woman did *not* get to ask about the children. She might have plans to play house with Ben, but the children were not part of the deal. Gina ignored the question, homed in on the angelic face and said, "Ben doesn't need your help anymore."

"Did he tell you that?"

Gina forced her voice to remain even. "*I'm* telling you that."

She might as well have said *Today is Tuesday and the sun is shining* for as much reaction as she got. "I respect your decision—" Emma shrugged, worked up a half smile "—but it's not your choice to make."

"Really? Whose choice is it?"

The smile inched further, spread until it exploded. "We both know the answer to that one." A dip in her voice, almost a caress. "It's Ben's."

"I hired you, Emma, not Ben. *I* paid for the extra visits insurance didn't cover." Gina coated her next words with extra sugar, shoved them out. "You've helped him regain his mobility *and* his life." More sugar and an extra squeeze of lemon at the end. "Thank you. Ben's made such progress, and he'll continue with swimming and a monitored exercise program, but you won't be part of it."

Emma Hale's smile slipped, worked itself back into place. "You hired me to help Ben and I delivered his recovery to you. He's moving, walking, even jogging, and his mental state is strong." Her voice dipped. "Better than ever. We've developed an emotional connection through his recovery and I don't think he's going to want to give it up."

Was this woman for real? "Excuse me?"

"I think you don't want to admit the obvious issue here." Emma sat back, crossed her arms over her nonexistent middle. "We both know we're not talking about Ben's physical recovery. We're talking about the emotional one and the fact that he's realized he doesn't want to be caught in a trap of obligation."

Gina skewered her with a look. "That's our marriage you're talking about."

A shrug, a sigh. "Why would you want to keep him like a caged animal? If you love him, why can't you set him free?"

Gina homed in on the woman, searched for the truth and the lies in her words. *Had* Ben told her he felt trapped? Had he said Gina was an obligation he wanted to extricate himself from as soon as possible? "Did Ben tell you that?"

"He didn't have to… He didn't have to say anything. Not directly. It was all in the faraway expression and the passion in his voice when he talked about the past, and the weight of his words when he spoke of the present. You've done this to him, Gina, forced him and tried to tame the wild spirit that lives in his soul."

"How dare you! You have no right to speak of my husband at all."

Emma raised a brow." Don't I? Don't I have a right? *I* saved him, Gina. *I* brought him back to life, not you. Do you really want to remain in a relationship with a man who's staying out of obligation? Shouldn't it be about love?"

"Get out." She sucked in a breath, spat out, "And stay away from my husband."

"I think I'll let that be Ben's choice." Emma Hale stood, grabbed her jacket, shrugged into it. "I hope you understand, this is nothing personal. I like you, Gina, you're a really nice person, but I'm not so sure you and Ben belong together."

Gina pointed toward the door. "Good-bye, Emma."

"Okay, I'm leaving. Just ask yourself this: why is Ben in

Philly?" She waited for Gina's response and when none came, she smiled. "Exactly. I think we should let Ben decide where he wants to be and who he wants to be with, don't you?"

~

LATER THAT NIGHT

Ben couldn't wait to get home.

He'd talk to Rudy Dean first thing in the morning, push for a start time to return to work, and he'd take whatever Rudy gave him, even if it was handing out flyers or a trip to Renova for paper products. He picked up his phone, dialed Gina's number. They had a lot to talk about, or maybe he should say *he* had a lot to talk about because he'd been pretty much stone silent since the accident. But not anymore, and he'd start with an apology for being such a jerk. When the call went into voicemail, Ben listened to his wife's voice as equal parts calm and agitation claimed him. Why wasn't she picking up? He checked his watch, calculated what she might be doing. It was almost ten... Was she asleep? Passed out on the couch from overwork and exhaustion? Maybe she was in the basement doing laundry and didn't hear the phone.

When was the last time she had a good night's sleep? How would he know when he hadn't slept beside her since the accident? And why was that? Ben dragged a hand over his face, let out a curse. Oh, right. He needed the benefits of a hospital bed with its height and sturdiness, and the stairs had been an issue. But the stairs hadn't been an issue in a long time. And the benefits of a hospital bed? That was such crap. What about the benefits of sleeping beside his wife? Feeling her soft skin, listening to her even breathing? Working up the damn nerve to make love to her again?

Damn, that last one slithered through him so fast it pinged his brain. *Fear*, it hissed. *Fear stopped you.*

He'd never disappointed a woman in his life—not in bed anyway, and he hadn't wanted to disappoint his wife. What if he struggled to move? Turned clumsy? Became so preoccupied with the what-ifs that his *equipment* refused to work? What then? He sucked in a deep breath, swiped the sweat from his forehead. Gina had tried to relieve his concerns even though he'd never mentioned he was worried about *that*. But she knew, he could tell by some of the comments she'd made. *I love you, Ben, we're in this together.* Or *Please don't overthink every part of your life. You'll be fine.* And then, a tiny smile that told him she was thinking about their sex life, followed by a soft *Better than fine.*

But he hadn't believed her because he had too much time to feel sorry for himself. That's what pulled him and Gina apart, widened the gap of intimacy until sharing a bed and sex with each other was past tense, and it had nothing to do with ability. When he got home, the first thing he'd do would be to pull Gina against him, kiss her with all the pent-up emotion he'd kept hidden these past months, and beg her forgiveness. Then he'd take her to bed—their bed—and confess his idiocy and yes, damn it, the *many* fears that plagued him since the accident.

Life would be good, like it was before he'd gone on a pity party of self-absorption, doubt, and fear. He missed Alex and Ava, too. Oh, they'd been there, but *he* hadn't. Nope, he'd been miles away, caught up in questions of mortality, life, death, the purpose of it all. He'd been so consumed with not dying that he'd stopped living. Not anymore. Once he hit

Magdalena, he'd scoop his wife and kids in his arms and thank God for opening his eyes to the real treasures in life.

He'd get another chance and he wouldn't blow it. Truth was, everybody would get old, gray, arthritic, less sharp, but what mattered was the now, and choosing the right people to take that journey with you. That's what really counted, and Gina was that person. Ben started to redial his wife's number when a knock on the door stopped him. Probably room service with the extra towels he'd ordered. "Just a second." Ben headed to the door, opened it. "Emma?"

Emma Hale stood on the other side of the door, tall, blonde, and smiling, a small suitcase clutched in her left hand. "Surprise!"

"What?" Surprise was not the word he'd use. *What was she doing here?* The smile spread, lit up her face as she stepped around him and entered the room. Ben turned, trying to understand why she was in Philly—in the same hotel. "Emma? Why are you here?"

She set her handbag and small suitcase on the end of the king-size bed and let out a small laugh. "You said you loved surprises and spontaneity, so I thought I'd give you a little of both." Those dark eyes sparkled. "I haven't gotten a room yet, but there are a few vacancies." Her voice trailed off. "I thought I'd check with you first and see what you wanted me to do."

What he wanted her to do was tell him why she thought she should be here and how she'd come to believe that talk of surprises and spontaneity meant with her. He hadn't been referring to her at all; he'd been talking in general terms, like a guy does when he's full of bullshit and has no intention or desire to do what he'd said. Had she thought he wanted to be *spontaneous with her*? No. Hell no. Ben stepped back, put distance between the bed and the woman who thought he wanted her there. He inched back further, shoved his hands in his pockets. "Emma, I think there's been a misunderstanding. I like you, you're a great person but..."

"But what, Ben? There's a chemistry between us that I can't deny, and I don't think you can either."

Chemistry? She was fresh air and sunshine with a can-do attitude and enough praise that made him believe he could do anything. That had pushed him through therapy, lightened his mood, and boosted his confidence. It also helped that she'd treated him like the starting quarterback on a Super Bowl team. Who didn't want to hear how great he was, how important? But that was all part of the bonding to help the recovery.

Wasn't it?

"Ben?" Emma moved toward him, her blonde hair brushing her waist. "You can be honest."

Honest. Yes, he could be, and she wasn't going to like it. "I'm sorry if you misinterpreted my intentions, but I'm married. I love my wife." The tears started, a slow trickle at first that picked up speed, made her swipe at them with both hands. *Crap*, he felt like a jerk for making her cry. Sure, he'd liked the attention she'd given him, more than liked it, but that was only harmless flirtation; he wasn't *interested* in her. He was only interested in his wife. How could she not know that? Had he sent mixed messages? That had never been his intention. Ever. Is that why Gina had been on him so much about Emma? Because Gina saw what he hadn't? Damn, but this was not good.

She sniffed, swiped at more tears. "I feel like such a fool. Why do I always end up with the wrong guy? When will I ever learn?"

He wanted to ask her how many "wrong guys" there'd been, but he hesitated. It was none of his business and he didn't want to deal with fresh tears, but he had to understand what was happening here—and what had happened before. "Emma, was the wrong guy a patient?" A quick nod, another sniff. "I see." And then he went after more details. "A married patient?" Another nod. "Are you sure you're not confusing the patient's gratitude and desire to get well with affection for you?" A shrug that could mean yes or maybe. "I know I was very grateful when you were there to help me. You boosted my spirits, made me feel like a king." He paused, gentled his voice. "But that's not real life and it's not a real relationship."

"But it could be, couldn't it?" More tears streamed down her cheeks, slipped to her chin and onto her blouse. "Oh, Ben, you are so beautiful and so perfect, and I know we could be good together. We're in sync, from our love of Thai food to our connection to Philly. And we're both athletes." Her lips pulled into a soft smile. "Your eyes light up when you laugh, sparkle and turn so blue my heart swells and all I can think of is you. I didn't mean to fall in love with you; it just happened."

She was in love with him? The woman didn't even know him, not really. Just because she'd helped him recover and they shared a city and the love of Thai food did not mean she knew him. If she did, she wouldn't be in this room right now telling him some BS about how his eyes sparkled. No, she wouldn't be here because she'd know he loved his wife and would *never* betray her. He had to make her see that whatever she'd imagined might happen between them was a one-sided fantasy and falling for her patients was a definite no. "Emma, look, I'm sorry if I gave you the wrong impression, but when a guy's hurt and suffering, he's not thinking straight because he can't get past his own misery. But that's not who he is and while he might complain about his wife or his sorry situation, even toss out a thought or two about how life's passing him by, at some point, he's got to stop whining and when he does, he realizes he wouldn't change a damn thing." He held her gaze, willed her to understand that physical therapy did *not* mean mental and emotional therapy. "The job of a physical therapist is to get his body back to a new normal, whatever that is, so he can accept it and move on with his life. *His* life, Emma, the one with the wife and kids who are his world."

Those dark eyes glistened with more tears. "But we connected, Ben. You know we did."

Connected? "If you mean you knew how to get me to care about doing those damn exercises and stop feeling sorry for myself, then sure, we connected." He rubbed his jaw, studied the tear-streaked face, the quivering lips. "But I thought that was your job."

"It *is* my job. But the emotional connection? The motorcycle talk, the memories of Philly, the prodding to live your life full-out?" Her voice slipped to a whisper. "That was for you, Ben, and not because you were my patient." More emotion spilled out, testimonies and pledges of a misguided heart. "I don't bake lasagna for just any patient's family, or inquire after the kids, but I wanted to get to know about Alex and Ava because I hoped one day I might be something more than just the woman who helped their daddy get better."

"Something more?" Ben narrowed his gaze on her, tried to ignore the tightness in his chest. *Did she think she could replace Gina?*

A dull red swept over Emma's pale face. "I had hopes."

Ben had heard enough; it was time to stop whatever fantasies Emma had conjured up that included him minus Gina. "That is *not* going to happen." He didn't try to hide the stern tone when he added, "Ever."

"Ever is a long time." She gathered up her handbag and small suitcase from the bed and made her way to the door. "I should probably say I'm sorry for all of this, but I'm not." Pause, a squaring of shoulders and a firm "I love you, and I won't apologize for that."

He doubted she knew what love was, but if she wanted to believe she loved him, so what? Her profession of love wasn't going to change anything. In fact, it opened his eyes to just how much crap he'd put Gina through by not listening to her concerns about Emma's interest in him. "I think it's best if I finish therapy with someone else."

"If that's what you want." She opened the door, turned back to him. "My feelings won't change, but maybe yours will."

"No, they won't." A mix of unease and anger squeezed his gut. He didn't like Emma's continued love talk or the implication that his feelings for her could change.

A shrug, a soft smile. "So long, Ben. I'll be seeing you." One more smile. "And about the therapy, Gina relieved me of my duties today. Guess she didn't like how close we'd gotten."

"You talked to Gina?"

"I did. She called, said she needed to talk to me right away. Urgent, is how she put it." A sigh, a shake of her head. "I told her I was on my way out of town and didn't have much time. We met, she told me my services were no longer required, and I said it wasn't her decision. She didn't like that."

Ben stared at the woman who was becoming his worst nightmare. "Why would you tell her that?"

"Because it's true. And I think she figured I was heading to Philly, but she never straight out asked. I would have told her, but sometimes people don't like their worst fears put into words. Anyway, when you want to see me again, you have my number. I'll be waiting." One more smile, a wave, and then the door clicked shut behind the woman he'd once called a godsend who was now a nightmare. Ben grabbed his phone, redialed his wife's number. She answered four rings later.

"Yes?"

"Gina? Are you okay?" He didn't miss the strain in her voice, as if she couldn't get enough air to form words.

A small breath filled the line. "I'm fine." Pause. "Why are you calling?"

She didn't sound fine. *He'd* done this to her. "You sound tired."

"It's late. Ben. What do you need?"

"I miss you. I'm sorry for putting you through hell." He wished he could see her face, touch her. "You were right about Emma." No response. "I should have listened to you when you said she was interested in me."

"It was obvious to everyone but you."

That sarcasm sounded a bit like the old Gina. "Guess I can be a thick-headed idiot." He waited for a laugh or a sarcastic comment, but all he got was silence. Ben cleared his throat, tried another tactic. "I've learned my lesson. No doubting you from now on."

More silence.

"Gina? Say something."

"What is there to say, Ben? Should I be upset she followed you to Philly? Or that she made us both look like fools?" Spurts of anger shot through the line. "You chose to believe a woman you'd just met over your wife and you're surprised I was right?"

Okay, he got it; he'd been a jerk. "I sent her away." Another silence. "Did you hear me, Gina? I sent her away, told her I loved my wife and kids, and whatever she thought she felt for me was a fantasy." He decided to leave out the part about how she said she'd be seeing him again, or how her feelings for him wouldn't change. No sense fueling Gina's anger.

"Well, I will certainly give you an *A* plus for the phone call." Her words slithered through the line, wrapped around his throat, squeezed. "Common sense? You fail."

Ben clutched the cell, sat on the edge of the bed, and let out a sigh. Could Gina not give him a little credit? Maybe not make it so damn hard to admit he was wrong and she was right? He tried again. "I *did* fail, but I won't fail again. I'm really sorry. I've had time to think and I just want to come home. I want to be with you." Time to open his heart and let out the truth. "I love you, Gina. I've always loved you even when I acted like I didn't care." Ben pictured her dark eyes, bright with emotion, full lips parted, arms open for him. More truth spilled out and this time he didn't try to hide the desperation lodged between the words. "I can't wait to come home, back to us." Life would be good again, things between them would get back to where they should be: together, a partnership. Why hadn't she responded? "Gina? I said I'm sorry and I love you, and I can't wait to come home."

"Yes, yes, you did."

His voice faltered, filled with uncertainty. "Don't you have anything to say?"

Dead silence filled the line seconds before she spoke the words that snuffed out his world. "What else could I have to say other than the truth? It's too late, Ben." *Click.*

And then she was gone, taking hope and joy with her.

10

Gina carried the suitcase and duffel bag down the steps and set them by the front door. He would be here soon, if the numerous phone calls and messages he'd left were any indication. Of course, she hadn't answered. What did she care that he had an epiphany, that he'd professed to love her with every breath in his body? Had he really said that part about the breath? Yes, that's what the second-to–the-last message had said. Well, too little, too late. Why couldn't he have told her that at any point these past few months when she'd been trying to help him? Why had he continued to shut her out, favoring Emma Hale instead?

Now he realized he'd been wrong?

How did she know nothing had happened between Ben and Emma? The woman certainly acted like it had, from the possessiveness in her voice when she talked about him to the way she carried herself—as though she had a right to the man, because they shared a secret bond—one that did not involve Gina. That could only mean sex. How could it not?

Ben swore nothing happened, but people lied all the time.

Maybe he was lying, too. Why couldn't he have let Gina help him? Why did he have to push her away? His constant rejection had led her to desperation and the enlistment of Emma Hale as his therapist—Gina's biggest mistake—the one that could destroy their marriage.

Now what? Should she give Ben another chance? But what if he *had* cheated? Once a man strays he can never be trusted again. Oh, some said he deserved another chance, that circumstances and situations created the unfortunate choice and somehow, somewhere, the offended party should find the strength to forgive and move forward. She'd always believed she and Ben would raise Alex and Ava, side by side, best friends and partners. They would be one of the lucky ones like Tess and Cash, Nate and Christine… And now Bree and Adam.

But there was nothing lucky about this situation, especially when she didn't know if she would ever trust Ben again. She'd never believed him capable of cheating, not after he pledged his love for her, shared in the birth of their children, whispered words of promise and forever. Maybe it was best to block those memories from her heart, erase them as though they'd never existed. As though the *man* had never existed or at least the part that claimed to love her. He would always be Alex and Ava's father, and if he chose to be involved in their lives, she knew he'd be a good father. But a husband? That was something she couldn't answer. Not yet.

❧

NEWS OF BEN and Gina Reed's uncoupling spread through town faster than the hailstorm that hit last week.

Cold.

Brutal.

Damaging.

Some said it couldn't possibly be true, not with two small babies and a love like Ben and Gina shared.

Others said it was a fabrication of the envious, and the fact that Ben now resided at Cash and Tess Casherdon's was a short-term situation of unknown origin and in no way linked to the "Angel" physical therapist, Emma Hale. Of course, there were those who disagreed. They were the ones who whispered that Ben and Gina were indeed separated and headed for divorce.

They were the ones who said the "Angel" physical therapist was at the bottom of it all.

Gina tried to ignore the sympathetic yet curious looks from her coworkers, the pauses, the stumbling sentences that started and stopped with *I know things will work out*, or *We're all pulling for you.* No one was brave enough to say whether *you* meant Gina solo, or *you* meant Gina as part of a couple— a Ben and Gina Reed couple. Emma continued her work at the hospital as though she were not the whispered third person in a love triangle involving a coworker and her husband. The woman shimmered with kind words and assurances for her patients and buckets of sympathy and smiles for Gina.

I really like you, Gina.

It's nothing personal.

Destiny comes when we least expect, but we must be ready.

When love presents itself, we have little choice but to listen.

And the most aggravating of all. *It just happened.*

How did a person handle such blatant disregard for a marriage? Gina had kicked Ben out three days ago, and word had it he'd camped out at Cash and Tess's. No secret there because Tess called her four seconds after Ben walked in the door with his suitcase and duffel.

Ben's here. What do you want me to do? Should I tell him he can stay or boot him out?

Tell him what you want.

What I want is to smack him across the face and tell him to wake up before he loses the best thing that ever happened to him.

Oh, Tess... Did you ever think he's already lost it and just won't admit it?

Please don't say that. Ben loves you, Gina. Pause. *And you love him. I know you do.*

Love causes pain and sadness, and there are no guarantees the other person won't hurt you.

He loves you, Gina. He's a mess. Cash said he's never seen him like this.

Gina pushed away bits of sympathy, replaced them with a coldness reminiscent of the woman she'd been before her husband walked into her life. *Maybe he should call Emma. I'm sure she'll console him.*

A gasp. *He says he never touched her, and I believe him.*

Of course, he'd told Gina that, too, but could she trust him to tell her the truth? She didn't know anymore and the fact that his ego and self-pity had put them in this position made her furious. Still, she couldn't pretend around the situation and expect it to go away. At some point, she had to formulate a plan.

On the sixth day of Gina and Ben's uncoupling, she visited the only lawyer she trusted, Bree's husband, Adam, and talked to him about a legal separation. After, she wondered if she should have waited longer to pull the thread that would escalate the unraveling of a marriage that had once been so good. Had emotion snuffed out the ever-logical common sense she'd always possessed, or was anger the culprit? Perhaps numbness? Exhaustion? Fear? Did she believe deep down that what had or hadn't happened between her husband and Emma Hale was a wake-up call to be proactive and minimize future damage to her heart?

As if anything could scorch her the way this mess had. There were moments when Gina wished she still lived in her safe world, away from hurt and loss, away from love. But that would mean she'd never have known what true happiness felt like, would not have held her children, looked into their eyes, heard her husband tell her he loved her. It had all been true and yes, it had all been worth it, even if the path led to an eventual break-up and a misery so great she knew she'd never be the same.

Adam had tried to tell her he was a corporate lawyer and didn't feel qualified to give her the best counsel regarding family issues. While that may be true, she'd bet it wasn't the main reason. No, that would have to do with not getting involved in the potential uncoupling of his wife's friend. Bree would no doubt be upset when she heard the news and pounce on her new husband, though something told her Adam could handle Bree without raising his voice, and chances were, she'd never know she'd been *handled*.

And that's why Gina had contacted him. The man had class, discretion, and intelligence. Besides, the agreement should be easy: no fuss, no confusion. It wasn't like she and Ben had Blacksworth-type assets or that she planned to keep the kids from him. It was about establishing boundaries.

A separation agreement was essential.

Ben did not agree.

He called her at work the day after Adam sent the letter

requesting a meeting to discuss a legal separation. "You talked to a lawyer?"

There was no pretending she couldn't hear the shock and frustration in his voice. Anger, too. And was there a tiny shred of fear tucked in at the very end? Gina sucked in a breath, clutched the phone. "Adam isn't just a lawyer." Pause. "He's a family friend."

Disbelief filled the line. "And Bree's husband. Gina, was this necessary? Could you not have given us a little more time? I told you I'd see a counselor, alone or together, whatever you wanted." Desperation trickled through the line. "I told you I'd do anything for a chance to save us." When she didn't respond, his voice cracked. "Or have you already given up?"

Had she given up? Her heart wanted to shout, *No, I will never give up on you. I will always love you, no matter what.* But her brain stopped her, forced out words meant to protect and keep her safe—from herself and the man who'd hurt her. "I need clarity, and this is how I can achieve it."

"By broadcasting to the whole town that you don't love me anymore? That you need a lawyer to tell me how to treat my kids and make sure I don't cheat you? I wouldn't do that, Gina." Pain laced his words. "I would *never* do that. I was a jerk who wallowed in self-pity and let anger consume me, but I never stopped loving you." His voice cracked, split open. "And I *never* cheated on you."

Gina pinched the bridge of her nose to keep the tears from spilling. Once they started, they might not stop. "You shut me out, Ben. You refused to let me help you and I was so desperate to see you recover that I..." She could not finish the sentence as visions of Emma Hale flitted through her head.

"I know." A long silence filled the line. "That's on me. If

I'd given you a chance, we'd be planning the summer vacation to Maine instead of talking about separation agreements." He let out a laugh: cold, harsh, empty. "I always was a day late in the relationship department. By the time I figured out what I should or shouldn't be doing, it was too late. But you were different, Gina; you challenged me, made me want to share. I never thought we'd find ourselves here, in separate houses—or separate beds. Some nights I dream you're beside me, so close I can feel you, smell your honeysuckle scent. Then I wake up." He paused, cleared his throat. Twice. "And when Tess's baby cries, I think it's Ava."

Oh, Ben...Ben... Her brain tried to sterilize the emotion his words created, but her heart won out. *Could* she trust him again? Could they have a chance to recover what they'd lost? Did she even want to try? There was only one way to get those answers. "I need time, so I can process what I'm feeling. I can't do that with you here, or with the worry that you'll show up and try to force conversations I'm not ready to have."

"I...okay."

"And I want us to meet with Adam and put the separation agreement in place."

~

Fifteen weeks after the accident

It was a sad time in Magdalena.

When one of the town's favorite couples isn't living in the same house and there's a lawyer involved, it's never a good sign. Oh, the lawyer can call it a *legal separation*, whatever that means, but when he gets tossed in the mix, that means the couple has stopped communicating, and that means headed for divorce.

Mimi had heard so many tales about Ben and Gina's situation that some nights she couldn't sleep for worrying about it. Those two belonged together, and Mimi vowed she'd do whatever she could to help them realize it. If only Pop were in town. She sure could use a bit of advice, but he'd headed to California for a long visit and double cataract surgery. Of course, he hadn't known about the cataract surgery when he'd boarded the plane last month. No, he'd thought he was in for a three-week visit with his son and Ramona Casherdon, Tony's new wife. But the clouded vision and "halo" around lights landed him in the eye doctor's chair and a recommendation for cataract surgery. Those eyes must have been bothering him for some time because Pop didn't fight too hard. Mimi called him once every three days to update him on the town happenings, especially the unfortunate events between Ben and Gina.

Pop didn't like to hear about that, not at all. He called Emma Hale an *interloper* and said Ben Reed wasn't the first man to turn fool from an overblown ego and too many buckets of self-pity. And Gina? He had a lot to say about her, beginning with *Why would that girl ever hire a looker like that* and ending with *Gina meant well but she sure had blinders on.*

Indeed, she had, but Gina's eyes were wide open now, and her attitude said she was not going to let anyone take advantage of her again—especially her husband. And that's why Ben was headed to the Heart Sent and his new temporary "home." When the doorbell rang, Mimi pasted a smile on her face and rushed to the door.

Ben Reed stood before her like a beaten shell of the young man who'd entered Magdalena more than four years ago.

Gone was the confidence, the attitude, the swagger, and in its place was a man who'd suffered his share of pain and sadness, even if most of it had been his own doing.

"Hi, Mimi." He stepped into the bed and breakfast he'd once called home, offered up a puny smile. "Thanks for letting me stay here."

"Oh, dear boy, you're always welcome." She hugged him tight, wished she could make the world right for him again. When she pulled away, she didn't try to hide the tears. "This is a sad state you're in, but we'll get you out of it, you'll see. One way or the other, we'll get you out of it." His eyes grew bright, too bright, and for a second, she thought she'd see tears, but then he cleared his throat and nodded.

"I appreciate it. I'm going to need all the help I can get to work my way out of the mess I created."

What to say to that? Ben had caused a lot of his own problems, and it wouldn't be easy to fix them, but he already knew that. "I don't have answers, but I do have a fresh pot of coffee waiting and a banana bread cooling in the kitchen." She laid a hand on his shoulder, offered up a smile. "How about we head on in and you can tell me all about what's going on between you and Gina?"

He nodded, his expression grim, the blue eyes that reminded her so much of her son's shifting to navy—a sign of worry and apprehension. From the first time Ben Reed swaggered into town with a boatload of arrogance and good looks, he'd reminded Mimi of her dead son, Paul. It wasn't just the dark hair, the blue eyes, or solid build. It was so much more: the hint of recklessness and determination, the lack of fear, the desire to take on whatever challenges crossed his way, even when the odds were against him. Well, the odds were against Ben right now if tales of his formal separation from Gina were true, and Mimi guessed they were. The news had come straight from Tess and Christine, who worried Gina might never trust anyone again, especially her husband.

Goodness, if that were the case, there was no hope left. Gina Servetti Reed had been raised by parents who chastised her for being intelligent and logical, preferring a picture-perfect size and shape. How did a person survive *that* without scars? But Ben had shown her he loved the person inside, that he didn't want a size two model as a partner. That boy had taught her that beauty was about more than a size and a shape; it was about strength, intelligence, loyalty, kindness, and commitment. Life had been good for them, almost perfect.

And then came the accident and along with it the fear that he might not be enough for his wife and children. His life *and* his dreams might have passed him by. That made him shut down, turn cold, and some said unfeeling, but Gina had not given up. Oh, no, she'd gone and tossed aside her own fears and brought on the one person who might bring her husband back to life. Emma Hale had been both savior and nemesis as she worked his body and gave him back a life —not his, but one she assured him would be filled with spontaneity and joy. *Living in the moment, living every moment,* she'd called it. But it was a misguided vision, one that did not fit a man with a family and responsibilities, and while it had seemed so exciting, it wasn't real—not for Ben.

Too bad he didn't realize this before he went to Philly.

Mimi had pieced the tale together from observation, comments from Gina's friends, and long-distance conversations with the wisest man she'd ever met: Pop Benito. *That boy's heading for a heap of trouble,* he'd said. *And if he doesn't wake up soon, he'll be worse off than a fly that's fallen in a bowl of sugar water.* In other words, Gina would only take so much before she called it quits and then, no matter what Ben did to try and fix his bad judgment, it would be too late.

That was not something Mimi could sit by and watch, not while she still had breath in her. She might have been unable to save her son, but Ben still had a chance, and with help and guidance, he *could* get his life back—the one he'd found with Gina before the accident scrambled his logic and his common sense.

Mimi made small talk while she fixed their coffee and sliced banana bread. The boy sure did love his sweets, and he'd been so good about keeping them out of the house to not tempt Gina. If only that girl could hold onto small memories like that, maybe she could work her way to the bigger memory—her husband loved her.

"So, guess you heard Gina and I are separated."

He said the word *separated* like he'd just bitten into a jalapeño pepper and it had burned his mouth. No sense pretending she didn't know about it when most of the town had heard the news. Hard to keep it quiet when one of Magdalena's most-likely-to-succeed couples was on the outs. Hearing about Ben and Gina's troubles was as bad as the tragedy that almost broke up Nate and Christine Desantro. And what about Cash and Tess Casherdon? Oh, she did not want to recall that sadness or how they almost lost each other—twice. Of course, Bree Kinkaid's widowhood misfortune had turned to pure gold when she found a solid man in her new husband, Adam Brandon, even if he had a lot to learn about the ways of a small town. Mimi sipped her coffee, tilted her head a bit so a dangle earring bobbed against her neck. "I heard, and I sure am sorry."

Ben shrugged, slathered butter on a slice of banana bread. "Who would have thought Gina and I would end up like this? One minute we're talking about Harry Blacksworth's Christmas party and guessing the number of trees he'll have in the house, and the next, I'm flat out in a hospital bed with a busted knee and a life I don't recognize."

Mimi reached across the table, patted his hand. "I understand how hard it must have been for you. Here you are, unable to use the body that was more machine than human, the one that had never failed you, and yet, now it didn't work." Another pat, a soft "That must have been devastating and if we can be honest, depressing." The slight nod he gave her said that was exactly how it had been. "Factor the emotions and the mental state with the physical limitations thrust upon you and no wonder you lost your way. When all you have is time and hope begins to run dry, it's not a good place to be."

Ben pushed aside the plate, rubbed his temple. "That's no excuse, Mimi. I threw away the best thing that ever happened in my life. Why would I do that?"

She offered a gentle smile. "That answer's easy because I've been through it myself. Remember I told you my Roger disappeared right after we were married? Wandered off for ten days, left me thinking the worst. When he returned, he said he'd needed time to think, that fear had taken a hold of him, but he was ready to commit to me." She raised a brow. "What do you think I did?"

"Took him back?"

She shook her head. "No indeed. I booted his behind right out the door and for the next five months, he sent me flowers and notes begging for another chance. Of course, I ignored him, but those flowers sure were pretty, and the notes were so sweet. But I was determined to make him pay for humiliating me, and I didn't know if I could trust him to not disappear again. Then one day the flowers and notes stopped, and three days later, the divorce papers showed up. Roger said he loved me but realized I was never going to forgive him, so he was setting me free." Her voice wobbled. "That was a real wake-up call. I marched right down to Rusty's Bed and Breakfast and we never spent a night apart again."

Ben rubbed his jaw, said in a gentle voice, "That's some story, Mimi."

"It sure is. Fear made my Roger run and it was fear that kept him away. The same is true with you and Gina. She saw the fear, the uncertainty, the hopelessness that consumed you, and she was willing to do anything to help." Pause, a shake of her head. "No matter the cost to herself." Mimi pinned him with a stare. "Can you imagine how difficult it was for her to ask another physical therapist to work with you? She might as well have posted a sign that said, 'My husband refuses to work with me.' That either means she's a lousy therapist or there are problems in the marriage. Again, for someone like Gina to have those possibilities exposed, especially in a place where she's well respected?" *Tsk-tsk* and a swipe at a tear. "That is devastating."

Mimi's words bleached the tan from his face, left him pale as paste. "I was too busy with my own tragedy to think about what it was doing to her. The more she tried, the more I pushed her away."

"Ah, yes, because she knew too much about the real you. The testimonial woman is what I call it. She's the one who's picked up the underwear, witnessed the bad moods, argued over the money, and seen the flaws, yet loved you despite them. And then along comes someone who's bright, fun, and free, doesn't know or care about your real problems or your backstory. No indeed, because that's *real* life and she's not interested in that. She is, however, ready to step in and tell you how perfect and wonderful you are, how grand life could be—*with her*." She raised a brow, patted his hand again. "Sound about right?"

"I never cheated on Gina, never even thought about it." Ben's voice split open with raw pain. "Never, Mimi, I swear on Alex and Ava's life. It was ego crap and looking forty in the eye, wondering if life had passed me up and the body had given out. I never cheated on her; you have to believe that."

She did believe him, but that was not really the point. "It doesn't matter what I think, Ben. It only matters what Gina thinks."

11

Ben went back to work the day after he moved into the Heart Sent. Rudy Dean gave him desk duty that included returning phone calls, typing reports, filing, and researching the specifications for the new booking room Rudy wanted built in the station house. All welcome tasks, even the follow-up calls about noise levels and a missing cat. If he stayed busy, he didn't have time to sit around and think about all the ways his life had imploded since the accident, most of it by his own hand.

Mrs. Olsteroff sat several feet away, her gaze darting toward him when she thought he wasn't looking. Oh, he was looking all right, taking in the pinched lips, the rigid posture, the clenched fists that said *not happy* and *how could you?* She wasn't the first person to cut him the evil eye, but most had done it in passing, while Mrs. Olsteroff shot him the look at ten-second intervals. After the fifth round, Ben sighed, tossed his pen on the desk, and homed in on the woman. "Do you have something to say to me?"

A burst of red spilled over her face, and she shook her head so fast her curls bounced. "No, I do not."

Another sigh. "Okay then. How about I do the talking and you do the listening?"

More pinched lips, a huff. "If you wish."

"I do wish. I'm guessing you're wondering what's going on with me and Gina." More red splashed her face, spread to her neck, a sure sign that was exactly what she'd been thinking. "Let me give you the short version. I screwed up and I'm trying to fix it."

Her face crumpled, her bottom lip quivered. "So it's true? You and *that woman*?"

"No! No, absolutely not." Ben sucked in a breath, fought the ache in his chest. "I would never do that to Gina. Do you hear me, Mrs. Olsteroff? I love my wife." Pause, a soft "I love her."

Ben realized a week later that it would take more than a profession of love and an apology to win his wife back. He'd visited the kids, tried to make small talk with Gina in the hopes it would lead to bigger talks, but she'd shut him down fast and disappeared into another room, leaving him with good intentions that didn't amount to anything.

Something had to change and maybe he needed an outside opinion or two on what that something might be. Cash and Nate could help him and that's why he'd asked for a meeting, and why they were sitting in the Casherdons' kitchen right now, drinking beer and eating nachos. Ben sipped his beer, shook his head. "How the hell am I going to get out of this mess when Gina won't say more than two words to me?"

Cash picked up a nacho, cheese dripping from it. "If you'd listened to me we wouldn't be having this conversation. All you had to do was man up and stop acting like a baby, and you'd be home sleeping in your own bed right now with Gina beside you." Cash plopped the nacho in his mouth, chewed. "And I wouldn't be here trying to rationalize your behavior to my wife—" he took a pull on his beer "—who, by the way, is not exactly thrilled with you right now. I'm sure I'm not the only one catching grief. How about you, Nate? Christine have any comments about husbands and their less-than-stellar behavior?"

"Christine hasn't come right out and said, 'Don't you ever be a fool like Ben Reed,' but the implications are there. Whenever Ben's name comes up or talk of a situation with a couple in trouble, she slices me a look, says in that soft sophisticated voice of hers, 'I'm sure glad we don't have these problems' or 'I know you would recognize when to come to me' or 'Please don't ever put us in this situation.' It's a real pain in the ass to get linked to a guy whose decision-making capabilities have taken a nosedive." Nate shot him a look that reminded Ben of the days before he and Nate Desantro were friends...back when they were almost enemies and Gina was a sore subject.

Ben toyed with his beer, thought about making a case for his less-than-acceptable behavior, decided against it. How could he argue that he hadn't been a jerk when they all knew straight out that he had? Worse, he'd pushed his wife away and refused her help. And why had he done that? Because he was an idiot, and later because the Savior Angel, Emma Hale, descended upon him with hope and promises and a bag of phony accolades that let him believe he was king of the planet. Right. The woman had some warped ideas on helping that included boosting her patients' egos and pretty much encouraging them to be self-centered jerks. The smiles, the aren't-you-wonderful comments said she believed he could do anything. What a bunch of BS!

Sure, Gina might not have given him extra stars for doing his therapy—okay, she would have burned him with a look and a command to get his butt moving, but he hadn't wanted that truth. Nope, he'd wanted someone to coddle him, tell him he was wonderful, make him believe he could be as strong and forceful and invincible as the pre-accident Ben Reed. The longer he had to think about recovery, the more he questioned his ability to be as good as he was before. There'd been no listening to Gina, even when he knew she was right.

Ben blew out a long sigh, let out a curse. "I'm sorry you guys are getting crap because of me, but I'm pretty pissed at myself right now, so you aren't alone."

Nate laughed, set his beer on the table. "Are you really going to give us the damn pity-party routine again? I thought you were over that. Maybe you really are a weak pain in the ass because the Ben Reed who rolled into Magdalena all those years ago would never lie down and give up, and he sure as hell wouldn't feel sorry for himself."

"Damn straight." This from Cash, who nodded and folded his arms across his chest. "That guy would swing first and ask questions later, and he would never give up on the life he wanted or the woman." Pause. "He definitely would not give up on the woman."

Were they crazy? Did they not understand Gina had filed for a formal separation, that he lived in one of Mimi's rooms right now, that she'd taken pity on him and fed him every night? That he didn't know if he'd ever sleep in his wife's bed again? If he'd ever make love to her again? Hell, he didn't know how long she'd *be* his wife. "I'm not giving up; I'm being a realist."

A snort from Cash. "A realist, huh? Sounds pretty touchy-feely to me."

"Shut up," Ben spat out. "What's wrong with opening my eyes and admitting the truth? Gina doesn't need me and maybe she's finally realized that."

"Oh..." Cash laughed. "Maybe she's finally realized that you *are* just a pretty boy with a pretty face and *she's* the smart one? I kind of think she knew that all along but loved you anyway."

"Go to hell." Ben scowled, clenched a fist to let Cash know he could still throw a decent punch.

Nate hid a smile. "Cash does have a point. Gina's a smart girl, and she loved you despite your many issues. Hell, let's be honest, our wives are all better than we are, and we don't deserve them, but that doesn't mean we're giving them up. If they love us, then we're going to damn well cherish that and protect it, no matter what." He homed in on Ben, held his gaze. "Right?"

"Right," Ben bit out.

"Well then," Nate said. "I guess we better come up with a plan before Mimi boots you out because you're not moving into my house."

EMMA SLID into a downward dog pose, tried to focus on her breaths, the soft exchange of air swirling about her as her chest rose and fell. *Calm...calm...* The external world faded away, the worries, the unknown...the confusion...all evaporated with those breaths. Peace and comfort settled in, washed through her arms and legs, her heart...reached her brain. And burst apart in a jumble of uncertainty and confusion. She tried to refocus, but it was no use. Emma eased out of the pose, blew out one last breath, and grabbed her water jug.

Why hadn't Ben reached out to her yet? Why was he waiting? She knew about the separation and the living quarters at the Heart Sent, knew too he was back at work, and she even knew he still visited his old house. Why wouldn't he go to the place where his children lived? A kind, compassionate person like Ben Reed would *not* ignore his children. He'd make sure he was a part of their life, and that's why he spent time at the house, not because he wanted to see his estranged wife. There'd been whispers in the department and about town claiming he was desperate to get her back, but Emma didn't believe them.

She *couldn't* believe them.

Ben just needed time to understand what his new life would be like: cross-country motorcycle rides, visits to Philly, maybe a jaunt to Chicago. If he could imagine it, why couldn't it happen? Life was meant to be lived full-out, no fears or regrets.

And Emma knew in her heart that Ben Reed was meant to spend his life with her.

It was this knowing that drove her to seek him out at the Heart Sent one evening. She'd knocked on the door of the bed and breakfast, and when Mimi Pendergrass opened it, the woman didn't try to hide her disappointment or her disapproval. "Emma? Why are you here?"

"I've come to see Ben." Emma peeked around the other woman's shoulder, tried to see inside. "Is he here?"

Mimi blocked the entrance, fisted her hands on her hips,

and stared. "He is, but I don't think he cares to see you." Pause, more staring. "Haven't you caused enough trouble for that poor man?"

Why did people always blame the third party on a relationship gone wrong? Didn't they understand there was trouble long before that person became involved? If Ben were truly happy and Gina were truly giving, then no amount of outside interest would create a fracture between the couple. But he *wasn't* happy, and Gina *wasn't* giving. Why couldn't anyone see that and why didn't Ben and Gina just admit it? "Mimi, I won't apologize for making Ben open his eyes to how life could be."

The woman shook her head, dangle-ball earrings brushing her neck. "How life could be? You've given that boy back his body and broken his soul. I welcomed you to our town, believed the stories that said you were a gift sent from heaven to heal." More head shaking, a pinch of lips. "But you took what wasn't yours, and you preyed on an injured soul, and there is no forgiveness for that."

No, that's not what happened. "I healed him, Mimi. I gave him hope." *Why couldn't these people understand?* "How do you think I did that? I had to make him *care* about something, and if that something was a motorcycle or a trip to Philly, so what?"

Those blue eyes narrowed on her, spit fire. "So what? So you manufactured discontent and then you fed it."

"I helped him see the truth."

She let out a harsh laugh. "The truth? My dear, you don't know the meaning of that word. I'd like you to leave, and speaking of truth, this whole town wants you to leave." Pause, a firm "The sooner the better."

Emma held the woman's gaze, visualized snow-capped

mountains, fresh-morning dew, and blue skies. Calm settled over her, brought out a smile and the mantra that had carried her through these past weeks. "Ben just needs time, and he'll see how good life can be."

"Oh?" Mimi raised a brow, tapped a finger against her chin. "With you, I presume? You'll show him that his world will shine brighter because of you?"

Emma's smile burst wide open. "Yes. Exactly."

More finger tapping against her chin. "Do you know the meaning of the word *delusional*? Because if you think that boy is going to take one step near you, then you *are* delusional."

Emma opened her mouth to respond, spotted Ben moving toward Mimi. "Ben?" She glanced around Mimi's shoulder, waved. "I need to talk to you."

He eyed her, the handsome face she'd memorized, unreadable. "Then let's talk."

Mimi Pendergrass looked up at him, clasped his arm. "No, do not speak with this woman. She has nothing you could want to hear. Don't do it, Ben."

He placed a hand over Mimi's, smiled at the older woman. "It's okay, I've got something to say to Emma, and now's as good a time as any." His voice gentled. "Will you give us a few minutes? This won't take long."

The woman hesitated as if she thought a man like Ben might require her protection. "I'll be in the kitchen if you need me." She nodded, shot one more look at Emma, and then disappeared down the hallway.

Ben motioned Emma to follow him into the sitting room. She remembered it well, especially the coffee table displaying photo albums of couples who'd honeymooned at the Heart Sent. Mimi Pendergrass had opened one of the albums, flipped through several pages, pointed at the couple smiling back at them. It was Ben and Gina Reed. Oh, but Emma had thought him so handsome, but nothing like the flesh-and-blood man, whose blue eyes and full lips could make a woman forget he wore a wedding ring. Emma darted a glance at the ring on his left finger, wished he'd stuck it in a drawer. "I've been trying to reach you."

Those blue eyes turned cold. "Sit down, Emma. We need to talk." He remained standing, hands shoved in his pockets, gaze narrowed on her as she slid onto the couch, smiled up at him. "I think there's been a misunderstanding and I want to set it straight." Those blue eyes shifted to black. "I love my wife and if I'm lucky, I'll have a life with her. But even if I don't, if she decides to press for the divorce, there *is no us*, Emma. You and I will never be together."

How could he say that? Emma sprang from the couch, moved toward him. "Please don't talk like that. Everything I've done I've done to help you, to give you a chance; surely you can see that."

"A chance?" His voice rumbled with what sounded like anger. "A chance to have a life again, or a chance to have a life with *you*?"

"Both." She reached out, touched his arm, ignored the flinch. "Ben?"

He shook her hand away, stepped back. "You have no right to expect that. Listen to me; I'm not going to be with you. I never wanted to be with you."

She blocked his words, pushed out dreams of love, hope, and understanding. "We can be good together. We can do anything we want; can't you see that? I'll ride anywhere with you. Do anything. Be anything. Free and fun with no boundaries."

He stared at her as though he couldn't understand her. "That's never going to happen. *Real* life isn't about no boundaries. It's about owning up to responsibility and finding a person you care about, and Gina's that person."

"I could be that person." Her voice slipped to a whisper. "I *want* to be that person."

"Why would you want to be with someone who didn't want to be with you?"

The words suffocated her: harsh, painful, filled with so much accusation. Was disgust buried in there, too? No, it couldn't be. Emma refused to believe it. "Because maybe you really *do* want to be with me, but just don't know it yet." She swiped at her cheeks, fought to keep more tears from coming. Why did all men hurt her like this? Why could they not understand the gift she wanted to give them?

"You need help, Emma. Professional help. There's something broken inside of you, something that's willing to reinvent yourself for a chance to belong to someone. Don't do that. You're worth more." His voice gentled. "Get help."

The tears fell and this time she couldn't stop them. She buried her face in her hands as her shoulders shook and her dreams fell apart. Life could have been good with Ben... Could have been perfect... Maybe it could still be perfect, but not until he understood what she was willing to do for love.

12

Spring swirled through Magdalena in gusts of wind and rain, making the residents wonder if they'd ever see warm weather. It had been almost six weeks since she'd kicked her husband out of the house. At first, Ben's absence had been a welcome reprieve. Having him around confused her. The anger and sarcastic comments he'd displayed after his accident were gone. She'd looked for them when he visited the kids, but no sense in hunting down something that had disappeared. What she saw now was the pre-accident Ben, the one who loved his family—loved *her*. This Ben fixed square and triangle peanut butter and jelly sandwiches for Alex and pulled giggles from Ava when he made funny faces.

This man could sneak past her defenses and crawl right back into her heart if she weren't careful. He might even be able to earn her forgiveness for what had happened these past months, including Emma Hale, and that's why she had to be careful. The hurt was still too new, the trust too shaky, the truth too unclear. She needed time and answers. What *had* happened between him and Emma, and why had he refused Gina's help?

There was more to consider, like the possibility that Ben could turn on her again. What if they found a way to salvage their marriage and suffered another misfortune? How would he react? Would he shut down, push her away? Turn to someone else? She would not open herself up to that kind of hurt again—not yet, maybe not ever.

When the doorbell rang, Gina opened the door to find Ben standing there, a pot of brilliant yellow tulips streaked with red in his hands. He held out the pot, his lips pulled into a faint smile. "For you."

She'd never seen tulips like this. The swirls of red against the yellow reminded her of fire, the pointed tips of the petals resembling the flame. "They're beautiful." Gina accepted the tulips, gestured for him to come in. "Thank you."

"I thought about roses, but tulips seemed more appropriate." He reached in his jacket pocket, pulled out a miniature toy car and laughed. "Another Mustang for Alex's collection." Ben rustled around in the other jacket pocket, pulled out a sweet potato. "And this is for Ava, because we know how she loves her orange veggies."

The tulips were a kind gesture, the car even more so, but the darn sweet potato? Priceless. It tugged at her heart, said Ava's father knew his daughter's weakness. Maybe he was trying to figure out Gina's weakness, too, or maybe he already had. "Well, feel free to use the food processor and whip up a batch for her." She studied the giant sweet potato, hid a smile. "That might get her through two meals."

Ben shrugged out of his jacket, nodded. "I'll let you know. Have a good time at Christine's."

"Will do." She hesitated, caught between the rush of

emotion at the thoughtful gestures and the need to protect herself from hurt. Protection won out. "I'll see you in a few hours." Then she grabbed her jacket, placed the pot of tulips on the front stoop, and headed toward the Desantros', away from the intensity in her husband's blue gaze that said, *Give us another chance. I won't let you down.*

Two days later, Ben found another angle to let her know he wasn't giving up. When he visited, he plunked a wad of cash on the kitchen table. "I thought you could put it toward a new garage door opener and whatever else you need. Mimi's not charging me for a room and I guess she thinks I'll starve unless she feeds me, so...."

Gina eyed the cash, slid a gaze toward Ben. "This really isn't necessary. The separation agreement was very generous." She paused, licked her lips, and added, "Very generous."

Hurt clouded his expression. "Take it, Gina. Please."

She hesitated, nodded. "Thank you." She'd put the money in a separate account in case he wanted it back. Money was not going to fix their problems and his next words said he knew that.

"It's only money, and it doesn't matter how much you have or don't have if you ignore what's important in your life. I... I've been thinking about the garden beds and know how much you've always wanted another perennial garden. Once the weather settles, I thought maybe we could get one dug out. I'd like to do it myself—" he pointed to his knee, offered a puny smile "— but I'm not sure I'll be up to it." He rested a hand on the table, leaned toward her, said in a gentle voice, "What do you think? Will I be able to use a rototiller and dig up a bed?"

His words made her chest ache. He knew she didn't care about jewelry, cars, or fancy clothes. Ben Reed, the man she married and gave her heart to, knew perennial gardens were her great passion. She cleared her throat, refused to get pulled in. "I think you should ask your doctor and your physical therapist."

"I trust your opinion more than anyone else's. *You* know my body, my strengths, and my limitations… You're a physical therapist, too." Those blue eyes glittered when he added, "And you're my wife."

Fresh pain tore at her soul, left behind shreds of what used to be. There was such regret in his words, such sadness on his face, that she wanted to tell him *Yes, I'll help you, I'll give you my opinion as your partner, your physical therapist, your wife.* But she couldn't do it. "This isn't a conversation I'm willing to have. We agreed you could come here to see the kids, but I won't have you pushing me."

He reached across the table, clasped her arm, his gaze fierce. "Does that mean we can't talk about it now, or ever?"

"I don't know, Ben. I just don't know."

His hand dropped, slid to his lap and for the briefest moment she saw a look she'd never seen in those eyes before: hopelessness.

BEN STOOD in the entrance of the physical therapy department, watched his wife and some tall doctor-type guy in a lab coat and bowtie engage in conversation. Too close, too many smiles, and what was the laughter about? Why would there be laughter in a physical therapy department where people were trying to regain their lives? He zeroed in on them, studied the body language. The doctor guy had a thing for Gina; Ben could tell by the sideways smiles and the expression that said he'd like to discuss more than ligaments, bones, and muscles. Maybe that's what they were discussing right now. Who knew? Ben sure didn't, but then he didn't know anything Gina was up to these days.

He shouldn't have tried to pin her down by asking if they'd ever be able to talk about their relationship, but damn, he was getting desperate. The more days that passed, the less he liked the odds of them getting back together. That's what made him open his big mouth and try to start a conversation, but Gina wasn't interested. The small talk they'd shared before ended the day he hinted at a timeline to talk. Now, when he stopped at the house to watch the kids, she pretty much ran out the door, no details on what she was doing or who she was doing it with, and after the first casual inquiry where she'd shot him down with a stern *You do not get to ask questions*, he'd shut up.

She was right. He didn't get to ask questions. Ben crossed his arms over his chest, leaned against the doorway, sucked in a deep breath. But that didn't mean he couldn't observe and draw conclusions or use his sources to track his wife's activities. He was a cop with analytical skills and deductive capabilities, and right now he was homed in on determining the relationship between Gina and the doctor with the bowtie and lab coat.

More laughter, add to that the guy's hand brushing Gina's shoulder, and that marked the beginnings of a potential relationship. Okay, Gina had stepped out of reach, but still, the guy had placed his hand on her. Had she backed away to *discourage* the familiarity? Or to hide the fact that they *shared* familiarity? He didn't know but he planned to find out.

"Ben? You ready?" Maggie Richot stood in front of him, clipboard in hand. She'd been his physical therapy assistant since he'd started the transition to squats with light weights and running on the treadmill—advanced training. One of the male physical therapists had drawn up his plan and Maggie implemented it. He would have preferred working with his wife, but she'd declined the offer. *You don't need my help*, she'd said, her voice tense. *There are a lot of other qualified therapists.* Well, maybe he didn't want other therapists. Maybe he wanted his wife.

"Sure." He darted one last look at Gina and the doctor and followed Maggie to the far end of the room.

"Why don't you warm up on the bike before we get started?"

Ben knew the drill, had gotten the go-ahead from the doctor last week to increase the strength training. He eased onto the bike, slid a glance in Gina's direction, noticed she and Dr. Tall and Smiling were gone. Where were they? "So, who was the guy in the lab coat talking to my wife?"

Maggie cleared her throat, turned three shades of red, and stumbled over an answer. "That's Pearson Taylor; he's the new orthopedic doctor who specializes in shoulder and elbow surgery."

"Pearson?" *What the hell kind of name was that?*

She smiled, shook her head. "He says it's a family name."

"I see." What Ben saw was old money—blue bloods, no doubt. Unlike him, who couldn't boast a father he knew or a mother who wanted him, which would make him a mongrel, wouldn't it? All he could lay claim to before Gina and the kids was a grandmother who doted on him and a big, fat chip on his shoulder. "He sure looked chummy with Gina." Damn straight he looked chummy and legal separation or not, Gina was still Ben's wife.

"I don't think he meant anything by it." Her voice dipped.

"Everybody knows she's had a rough time, and they're just trying to help."

She meant because he'd been a jerk and trusted a stranger instead of his wife. Ben pedaled faster, pictured Gina's dark head resting against Pearson Taylor's shoulder, her hands clasped in his. No. *Hell, no.* He blinked hard, dragged his gaze to Maggie's. "I owe Gina a lot more than an apology, and if she gives me a chance, I'll do my damnedest not to hurt her again." Pause. "Or be a grade-A jerk." He breathed harder, increased speed. "But I will not sit back and let my wife, the mother of my children, be sweet-talked by some guy named Pearson."

"Go after her, Ben. Don't let her get away."

Sweat beaded on his forehead, trickled to his temples. Ben pumped the pedals faster, jaw clenched, and thought of Gina and all the ways he'd hurt her.

"Ben." Maggie touched his arm. "Slow down, okay? This isn't a race. It's just you against yourself."

He eased up on the pedals, blew out a breath. "Right." Then he turned to Maggie, let her see the fear and uncertainty. "I know I don't deserve her, but I'm not giving her up."

"Good." Maggie squeezed his shoulder. "A lot of us are cheering for you."

∼

TWENTY-ONE WEEKS *after the accident*

Ben's SUV was the first thing Gina spotted when she pulled down the street. The pile of dirt was next. And were those Nate and Cash's vehicles? Sure looked like it. What was going on? If Ben had gotten it into his head to dig out a perennial flower bed, she would not be happy. He'd tried to talk to her about one a few weeks ago, but she'd changed the subject.

She opened the car door, made her way to the backyard and the clang of shovels and voices. Her husband pointed at a piece of paper, motioned toward a section of dug-out yard. Nate and Cash studied the paper, shovels clutched in their gloved hands. Clusters of flowers in pots and plastic trays lay several yards away, no doubt the new additions for what she guessed would be a perennial flower bed. Gina squinted, noticed bee balm, lavender, daylilies, and delphinium. Had Ben selected them himself or asked for help? Her annoyance at his high-handedness softened at the realization that he really had listened to her perennial garden wish list.

That lasted three seconds before the reason behind her annoyance resurfaced. Why did Ben think he could walk into the backyard and tear it apart? Even if it were exactly what she wanted, had talked about a new bed since last year? *You can't have a garden without lavender,* she'd told him. *And bee balm and daylilies. Not the plain yellow daylilies because everybody has those. I want different, stunning.* The burgundy and gold daylilies resting under the shade tree were indeed stunning.

But that was not the point. Ben did not have a right to decide for her anymore, even if his choices were what she wanted. They were separated and that meant apart, disconnected, divided. No sharing other than the children. Why couldn't he understand that she didn't want or need his help? Did he think she couldn't make it on her own? Couldn't hire out someone to dig a bed or ten beds if that's what *she* wanted? Gina thrust her hands on her hips, waited for her husband to notice her *and* her displeasure. Nate and Cash spotted her first, lifted a hand in greeting. Of course, Ben was too busy with his plans to notice her until she was steps away. "Ben? What are you doing?"

He swung around, the smile on his face slipping just a bit. "Hi, Gina. Surprise!" He moved toward her. "Nate and Cash have been helping me. It's your early Mother's Day present." He motioned toward the large circle of dug-out dirt that would become a perennial garden. "I wanted to have it done before you got home." He shot a glance at her, shifted from one foot to the other. "Aren't you a little early?"

"My last appointment canceled, and I thought I'd stop home before I pick up the kids. Ben, what is all of this?"

His brows pinched together in what looked like confusion and disappointment. "I told you, it's your Mother's Day present. I know it's a little early, but you've talked about it a long time, so I figured, why not do it now?" The words tumbled out, spilled at her feet. "I'm sure I didn't get all the flowers you talked about, but I thought you could go to the garden center and pick out the rest later."

Gina glanced at Nate and Cash, took in their rigid stances, the intense looks trained on her. Did *they* think this was a good idea? Couldn't Nate, Mr. Responsible, have guided Ben in a different direction, like maybe not-a-good-idea direction? "Am I the only one who has an issue with this?"

Cash shrugged, wiped a hand over his brow, smearing sweat along his forehead. "We thought it was a pretty good idea, seeing as how you love your flowers."

"Anybody can buy a piece of jewelry," Nate said. "But it takes a special person to find a gift that touches the other person's heart." His dark gaze narrowed in challenge. "Don't you think so, Gina?"

What to say to that? "Of course, it does, but gifts must be given *and* received with intent. And the other person's desire to *not* receive a gift should be respected."

Cash muttered a curse. "Oh, for the love of—"

"She's right." Ben yanked off his work gloves, slapped them against his leg. "I guess I really am a fool. Here I thought this would mean something to you, that asking my friends to help me and putting myself out there for rejection *once again*, would tell you how much I want us to work." His blue gaze burned her, but his next words opened new wounds. "I should have known this was a mistake because Gina Servetti Reed does not like to forgive when she's been hurt. She prefers to cut the offender out of her life and carry the hurt around as a reminder that most people aren't worthy of her love *or* her trust."

That wasn't true. She opened her mouth to tell him she knew how to forgive, knew how to start over and had done it with him, but this time was different. This time she'd known true joy, a belonging so deep it scared her. And the very person who'd given her that joy had ripped it away. Could she ever forgive that? Did she want to risk the pain and hurt of loving too much?

"Didn't think you'd have an answer for that one." He picked up his shovel, thrust it over his shoulder. "Just leave it, guys. I appreciate the help, but it looks like it's been a waste. I'll fill in the area and return the perennials, then Gina can do whatever she wants." He shot her a look, his gaze cold, the brackets around his mouth deep. "Maybe your doctor friend can give you a few suggestions; seems like he's more in tune with you these days than I am."

And with that, he nodded to his buddies and headed toward his SUV.

Cash blew out a long sigh. "Well, that was pretty bad.

Gina, can't you see the guy's trying to make things right? Why can't you cut him a break? Do you know how hard it is for him to beg?" He took a step closer, shook his head. "Guys like Ben have a hard time apologizing, even when they're wrong. He laid it all out in front of us and you pounded him in the dirt, shoved his face in your self-righteousness, and that is so wrong."

Gina blocked out Cash's words. She would not let him make her feel guilty when she was the injured one in this marriage, not Ben. Oh, he'd suffered a physical injury that had turned into an emotional one, but his refusal to let her help had damaged their relationship and created the perfect hunting ground for Emma Hale. Still, Ben's friends might not quite see it that way.

"Okay, Nate, it's your turn. Go ahead and spit it out. Tell me how unfeeling I am, and how I should forgive Ben for everything because he wants to dig me a flower bed." She laughed, because it was so much easier than crying. "Why could he not have done the right thing in the first place, so we wouldn't be here? Why could he not have opened himself up to me and let me help him as his wife, his friend and partner?" Darn, but her voice wobbled. "The person who cared about him more than anyone in the world?" The tears started, fat ones that slid down her face, slipped to her chin, onto her scrubs. "He let a woman he didn't even know destroy what we shared because he was afraid and didn't trust us, and you want me to pretend it never happened, pretend *she* never happened?" She swiped at her face, cleared her throat. "I can't forget it. Every time I look at him I see betrayal, and I don't know if I'll ever get past that."

Nate stepped toward her, touched her shoulder, and said in a gentle voice, "I know all about hurt and pain, and I'm sure my wife can tell you about feeling betrayed. But have you ever considered that while your husband's actions were misguided and foolish, he did not betray you? When I look at him, I recognize that man because I've been him. Torn with self-loathing because I knew my actions caused so much pain to the person I loved more than my own life, and there wasn't a damn thing I could do about it. How could I prove what I knew in my heart when the evidence was against me?" His voice shook with emotion. "There were photos of me doing things I knew I hadn't done, and yet I couldn't prove it. I never betrayed Christine, but that's not what those damn photos said, and look how it was all a lie? Wouldn't it be convenient if you ended up divorced and Emma Hale just so happened to show up to comfort him?"

"Did you ever think of that?" Cash crossed his arms over his broad chest, stared at her. "You could drive that damn woman right into his arms, and then whose fault would it be? He's here, he's begging, and trust me, for a guy like Ben, begging is not easy. If you turn him away now, you might as well file for divorce because you've already decided he's not worth it, and neither is the relationship."

Gina stepped away from Cash's words and the possibility that they might be true. "I haven't decided anything." She settled her gaze on the partially dug-out bed, pictured it bursting with perennial flowers that would grow and multiply over the years. "I never thought this would happen to us."

"Us?" Cash slashed a hand in the air, muttered another curse. "This is nothing, trust me. Try having some woman waltz into town and tell you a kid you didn't know existed belonged to you. And then try having that same woman make your wife believe it *was* true, make you question everything you know about yourself and your marriage. That friggin' woman came to town and told me she was dying, that Mason was my flesh and blood. How cruel is that, especially when Tess and I had been trying so hard to have a baby? You were there, you know what happened, but we fought through it..."

Gina nodded, said in a soft voice, "I always knew nothing would keep you and Tess apart; your love is true and strong. The same with Nate and Christine."

"But yours isn't? You think Ben's just passing time and wants to be a city boy again, without a wife or kids or anything to hold him down? Come on, Gina, open your eyes. Do you remember the crap I went through when I came back to town? Busted up, beat up, I didn't know who I was or where I was going. And Tess? She was a vision, a dream, and a nightmare all wrapped into one. I didn't want her sympathy, didn't want her help, and I damn well didn't want her back in my life because I was too busy feeling sorry for myself. I get the not wanting to trust again, because I've been there. I'm still pissed that Ben was such a jerk, but he's trying to make it right. The way I see it, it's got to come from you now. And something else." Those whiskey-colored eyes singed her. "You want to hurt him real bad, you keep talking to that pretty-boy doctor, and you won't have to worry about him bothering you anymore. One thing about my buddy is the day he realizes there's no more hope, he'll stop the bleed."

"Stop the bleed? What does that mean?" She didn't need Cash's explanation to dissect what he meant. He may as well have said *The day Ben believes there's no chance for a future with you will be the day he shuts down for good.* No, she didn't want that, but she needed time to understand what her world would look like if she and Ben were together again. Would they be stronger? Would they carry animosity and doubt in their hearts? Would they make it a year, maybe three, before they realized they didn't belong together? Her heart said *No*, cried *there must be another way*, but her brain badgered her with doubt. *Will you be enough for him? Will this happen again? If you open up, can you survive the pain if he hurts you again?*

She waited for Cash to continue his barrage, but it was Nate Desantro who laid it all out for her in simple words that left no doubt as to their meaning: no frills, no raised voice, nothing but the truth as he saw it—a truth that was straight on. "We all hurt each other, especially the ones we love most. But that doesn't stop us from loving that person or showing up every day and fighting for the relationship because life without that person in it isn't life at all."

13

Gina had avoided her friends for too long, choosing anger, hurt, and self-preservation instead of logic, hope, and empathy. After what happened this afternoon with the perennial garden fiasco, she needed guidance. She couldn't think straight, couldn't find a way back to the objectivity that had once claimed her decision-making processes. Cash's harsh words burrowed in her soul, but it was his warning that scared her. *One thing about my buddy is the day he realizes there's no more hope, he'll stop the bleed.* Nate's words were less stark, but just as chilling. *We all hurt each other, especially the ones we love most.*

Gina knocked on Christine and Nate Desantro's door, sucked in a deep breath. She'd contacted her friend this afternoon, asked if she might meet her, Tess, and Bree for what Gina had called a long-overdue intervention. What an understatement. When Christine opened the door, her smile and subsequent hug said that no matter the circumstances, they would always be friends.

"It's so good to see you." Christine gave her one more hug before she pulled back and welcomed her inside.

"Thanks, it's good to see you, too." Gina lowered her voice. "Are Tess and Bree here?" Tess wouldn't throw judgments or accusations at Gina, but Bree might. She and Ben had a special relationship that had seen her through the grief of a miscarriage and later, the scandal surrounding Brody's death.

"They're both here. Actually, Bree arrived early, can you imagine that?"

The comment about their friend's punctuality made Gina laugh. "Seems that new husband of hers has been teaching her a few things." Bree had been given a second chance when Adam Brandon walked into her life, but in what seemed to be a trend among these women, she'd almost lost him.

"They're perfect for each other." Christine's blue eyes sparkled. "Don't be surprised if one of these days there's not a baby announcement." Bree had vowed she was done with children and yet before the disaster that had become Gina's life, she had made a reference or two about adding to the brood, saying *Every once in a while, Adam and I talk about it, but how can we improve on perfection?* Yes, she and Adam had found perfection: they loved each other, he loved her children and was raising them as his own. They took trips to Chicago and Laguna Beach, had even talked about the Grand Canyon next year. Bree deserved this happiness and she'd finally gotten it with a solid man who would do right by her.

Gina followed Christine into the living room, took in the hardwood floors, stone fireplace, and comfortable furniture. It might not look like a place Christine Desantro would choose, but it fit her, just like her husband and the life she had in Magdalena. She and Nate had been able to work past differences that had seemed hopeless. So had Tess and Cash. Could Gina and Ben?

It had been so long since she'd visited her friends and she'd missed the honest conversations and sometimes not-so-gentle prodding that came with being a friend. Tess sprang out of her chair, threw her arms around Gina. "I heard all about what happened, and it didn't sound pretty."

Gina tried for a laugh, failed. "Pretty? It was downright ugly."

Christine placed a hand on her arm, squeezed. "And that's what we need to talk about."

"Indeed, that's exactly what we need to talk about." Bree's voice reached Gina seconds before the woman appeared from the kitchen carrying glasses and a bottle of wine. She set them on the coffee table, made her way to Gina, and pulled her into what she called a Bree-bear hug. "I am so sorry." Bree pulled away, her eyes filled with tears. "We have got to get this figured out, and soon. Ben loves you, and he would *not* cheat on you." Those amber eyes narrowed, and she spat out, "Not like that dead loser husband of mine. Ben worships you and while he might have taken a detour into self-pity and don't-know-where-I-am land, *you* are his very heart and soul." The full lips flattened, the brows pinched. "Emma Hale tried to paint a story but it's just a story and a bad one at that. We'll dig around and get to the bottom of this." More brow pinching, a scowl. "It's going to be as stinky as a dirty diaper, you can count on that."

Bree did not want to believe Gina might not get a happily-ever-after, considering she'd found her own with Adam Brandon. "I appreciate the visual and the kind words, but we both know this is about a lot more than bad story-telling and stinky diapers. It's about honor and staying the course and believing, no matter what. Ben gave up on *us* long before Emma Hale entered the picture." *That* was the part that still made Gina's heart ache.

"Cash is pretty upset with you right now," Tess said in a quiet voice. "He thinks *you're* giving up."

Giving up? Gina opened her mouth to tell them that her husband was the one who'd given up, but Christine spoke first.

"Nate's trying to see both sides, but in typical Nate style, he's more about loyalty and honor, but darn if he isn't into letting second chance have a shot." She tried to hide her smile, but it snuck out. "My husband has become much more forgiving than he used to be, and it's a very admirable trait in a man who did not believe in forgiveness *or* second chances."

Gina slid onto the couch, folded her hands in her lap, and darted a glance at her friends. "We've seen each other through a lot of sadness, even before Christine came to Magdalena, and we've never given up on each other. But I don't know how to get through this to find a way back to my marriage. I'm not even sure I can."

Bree sniffed, sat on the couch next to Gina, and clasped her hand. "I did not speak with Adam for half a day after I learned he met with you and Ben to file separation papers. I tried to tell him you two belong together, and he needed to stay out of it, but do you know what he did?" She stuck her nose in the air, let out a long sigh filled with annoyance and just a hint of disbelief. "That man told me to stay out of his business unless I had a law degree tucked in my dresser that he didn't know about. Can you imagine?"

Tess smiled. "That man is my true hero. Anyone who can stand up to Bree and tell her to mind her own business and mean it? Well, that man's a keeper, especially when he's married to Bree."

Bree lifted a shoulder, rolled her eyes. "Perhaps I was a smidgeon invasive with my comments, and perhaps it wasn't my place to state my concerns, but my husband did not need to rub my nose in it."

"Or perhaps he did." This from Christine, who offered a gentle smile and a persuasive, "You know Adam is an honorable man who cares about you and doing right by this town. You can't expect or ask him to jeopardize his principles to make you happy, can you?"

Another eye rolling, this one more dramatic than the first, followed by a sigh that lasted a full ten seconds. "I guess not. Besides, when Adam explained the law to me and how it worked, I understood." A tiny smile slipped across her full lips. "He did admit the separation agreement was hard for him especially when he didn't want to disappoint me and further, when he thought about Ben and Gina and their family and how much he respected them."

Gina nodded, admitted what she'd been hiding. "I didn't know what else to do to protect myself, or to let Ben know I was serious about not being played or taken advantage of again. Still, meeting with Adam and then bringing Ben into the office to talk about the specifics of money and visitation and what it could all mean… That was horrible." She remembered the disbelief on Ben's face, the bleakness, the despair. "I didn't want to cause him hurt or destroy our chances for reconciliation, but…"

"You didn't know what to believe and you weren't going to set yourself up for the pain his betrayal could cause you?"

Christine's words pierced her soul. Gina tried to fight the

tears, but it was no use. She swiped at her cheeks, cleared her throat, and managed a raspy "Yes."

"We want to help, but you have to let us." The commitment in Tess's voice said she would stand by her friend, no matter what.

Bree's words spilled over her next in a flurry of determination and promise. "You helped us and guided us through some rough times. Now we want to do the same for you but please, don't shut us out."

Gina wiped her eyes with the tissues Christine handed her. When she tried to speak, her voice wobbled, split open with sadness and uncertainty. "How will I ever trust him again? How can I believe him when that woman's words make me think what she said is true?"

"She-devils and witches cast spells that make us question ourselves and the loyalty of our husbands. Do not succumb to that evil witch's spell. You're strong, and you deserve the happiness of the man who loves you." Bree's words shook with conviction. "I almost let myself be destroyed by Brody's actions, and I was ready to toss away a good and loyal man like Adam because I did not want to believe in trust and love again. Maybe I didn't think I deserved it, or maybe I believed his less-than-honest reason for being in our town would end in another betrayal as bad as Brody's. That was pure foolishness on my part and if you all hadn't forced me to open my eyes, I might be living in regret and eating toasted cheese sandwiches six days a week instead of Adam's teriyaki salmon and grilled asparagus."

~

MEN HAD ALWAYS SHIED AWAY from Gina, saying she was too

much work, her mouth was too sharp, her wit too cutting. Of course, Ben had never shied away from her. In fact, when he first met her she'd annoyed him, but there'd been something about her, part mystery, part intrigue that created a fascination he wanted to solve. Once Gina opened up to Ben, Pop Benito said she bloomed like a hardy hibiscus: her beauty increased, her harsh comments softened, her confidence grew, made people do a double take, especially the men. They wondered how they'd ever missed such a delightful find: an intelligent woman with a sharp wit and the natural beauty that went with it. Of course, Gina didn't know or care what others thought. She was blinded by her husband and that rare and special love that comes from being with your one and only. That didn't stop male appreciation though none would ever act on it, not when there was zero chance of success and she had a husband who knew how to deliver a black eye.

But the situation had changed. Gina was officially separated from Ben and in some people's eyes that made her available *and* attainable. One person who'd been interested in her was Dr. Pearson Taylor, a man who'd grieved the loss of his wife in a drowning accident for two years and was ready to move on. Of course, the females of Magdalena had noticed him, and of course many had made their interest known, but the handsome doctor from Michigan had no interest in them. Oh, he was polite and cordial and he asked after their families, but his blue eyes didn't light up like they did when he saw Gina, and his smile didn't spread when he talked to them. No, those looks and smiles were reserved for Gina Reed.

Some people had noticed; some even suspected there was something going on between the two. There were even those who *hoped* something was going on, but those individuals were the ones who were after Gina's estranged husband, Ben.

Had Gina known or suspected the kind doctor's inquiries and laughs were anything other than casual interest and a desire for friendship, people said she would have clammed up and shut the man down so fast she'd freeze the smile on his face. But there were others who said, *Not so fast. Maybe Gina Reed's ready to move on and maybe Ben Reed isn't her one and only.*

But as in all things, time and circumstances would indeed tell. For now, Gina considered Pearson Taylor a friend and when he asked her to dinner on Thursday afternoon as they were eating lunch in the hospital cafeteria, it surprised her as much as it confused her.

"Pearson, we're eating lunch; I'm not so sure we need to have dinner together, too." She raised a brow, lifted a forkful of salad, and pointed it at him. "There are only so many ways to eat a salad."

He laughed, his dimples deep, his blue eyes sparkling. When the light shone on his eyes a certain way, they reminded her of Ben's eyes. Not as blue, not as intense, *not Ben's...* "Actually, I was going to suggest Harry's Folly. I hear they've got quite a few choices besides salad."

Harry's Folly. She and Ben had always loved the place, had chosen it for their anniversary celebration, his birthday... Gina wasn't interested in going to Harry's Folly with anyone other than her husband, but Pearson really was just a friend and she should be able to have dinner with a friend, even a male one, shouldn't she? She forked a hunk of romaine lettuce, plopped it in her mouth. Was she supposed to avoid every place she and Ben had enjoyed? No Harry's Folly, no

Lina's Café? What about the Heart Sent? Or visiting Pop Benito? Should she avoid all of them? Move out of Magdalena?

This was foolish. Did she really think she could obliterate what she and Ben had shared by moving to a different town? A different state? How about a different country? Her heart told her she would *never* forget him, that no matter what happened she would not be able to erase the memories. Would she want to...? They'd had four years of such pure joy and happiness. Why pretend it never existed because life chose a different path...because Ben decided life with her was too confining, *she* was too confining?

Oh, he'd told her he'd made a mistake, had been a fool, and sometimes she really thought she was ready to forgive him, but then she'd remember the hurt and pain he'd caused and she grew angry all over again. She never wanted to feel that pain again, and that's why she accepted Pearson Taylor's offer for dinner at Harry's Folly. They were friends and it was only a dinner; she knew that, and Pearson should know it, too. If he didn't, she'd make sure he did before the dinner was over.

14

"Vanessa thought about opening a restaurant. Said small and intimate was the way to go; encourages people to share and makes them want to come back." Pearson glanced around Harry's Folly, rubbed his strong jaw. "She would've done a great job."

Gina and Pearson sat in a booth at the back of the restaurant. The same booth where she and Ben usually sat. Quiet, intimate, away from chatter and curious onlookers. Had Harry seated them in this booth for a reason? She hadn't missed the extra-long look he slid her a second before he smiled, gave her a hug, shook Pearson's hand. *It's a busy night,* he'd said. *I'll see if I can get you some privacy.* She'd wanted to ask why he thought they needed privacy. She didn't need it, didn't want it, not when this was just a dinner with a friend. Was he trying to protect her from gossipers? Or was he trying to protect Ben from hearing his wife had dinner at Harry's Folly with another man?

Harry reappeared minutes later with the wine list and menus. "We've added a few new items to the list." He laughed. "I didn't like the idea of change, but Greta talked me into it, said you have to mix things up a little every now and then so people don't get bored. Huh." He rubbed his jaw, shook his head. "She was right, but then, my wife usually is." Another laugh, this one deeper, louder. "I told her she could change anything she wanted, just so she didn't change husbands." His face went pale beneath his tan, his blue eyes grew wide. "Damn, but I'm sorry, Gina. Me and my big mouth. Gets me into trouble every time."

Gina cleared her throat, shifted her gaze to Pearson who stared at Harry Blacksworth as if he were still processing the man's words *and* his intent. "It's fine, Harry. No harm done."

The paleness beneath Harry's tan faded, the pinched brows smoothed out. "Drinks on me. It's the least I can do for running my mouth. Just let me know what you want."

"Thanks, we will." Pearson turned to Gina, his handsome face a mix of disbelief and concern. "Is that okay with you?"

Had he just dismissed Harry Blacksworth, one of the kindest, gentlest men in this town? "Yes, fine." Gina turned to Harry, offered a smile of apology for Pearson's inconsiderate behavior. Harry might not always choose the right words, but his heart was pure, and he'd done more good for this town than most of the residents who'd been born here. Could Pearson not have overlooked the unfortunate comment? The forlorn expression on Harry's face said he'd carry this regret around all night if she didn't find a way to snuff it out. Gina chose the one tactic she knew that lifted every dog owner's spirits: sharing their animal's story. "Harry—" Gina placed her hands on the table, leaned toward him with a bright smile "—I hear there's a new addition in the Blacksworth house? Cooper, is it?"

Harry's face beamed at the mention of his dog. "Sure is.

That boy is something else. I found him on the back roads from Renova. Skinny thing, all alone...looking for a place to belong is my guess. Named him Cooper after Gary Cooper in *High Noon*. He sure is a lot of work." He shook his head, sighed, said in a soft voice, "But he's worth it. Just like most things in life, don't you think?" His blue eyes glittered. "Yup, dogs are a lot of work; sometimes they're downright messy and you want to quit on them, but you don't, because you can't. Your heart's already done; they stole it the minute you saw them and there's no going back now. Sure, I could say Cooper's too much work and he's not worth it, but then what?" Another sigh, this one longer, deeper than the last. "It's not like I'm going to go find another one like him because there *isn't* another one like him." He met Gina's gaze, held it, his smile slow, steady. "You know what I mean about those strays, don't you, Gina? Sometimes you can't live with them, but damn, you can't live without them. So, you make sure they're house trained, teach them the rules, and they're so grateful for it, they're loyal to the end." He looked at Pearson head on, gaze narrowed. "You got a dog, Pearson?"

The man cleared his throat, shook his head. "I do not."

"Well then, guess you can't understand." He shifted his gaze back to Gina. "How about you, Gina? Any dogs at your house? Maybe a stray?"

Pearson jumped in. "Gina doesn't have a dog." He glanced at her, added in a sheepish voice. "Do you?"

She shook her head. "No dog." She slid a look at Harry. "And no strays."

That made Harry laugh, a deep-bellied laugh that told her he knew exactly what he was doing and wanted her to know, too. The man wasn't talking about a four-legged animal; he was talking about Ben. "She used to," Harry added. "But she couldn't housetrain him and had to give him the boot. Still, I'm not sure she's given up on him yet."

Gina pinched her lips and gave Harry a look that was as close to a scowl as she dared with Pearson watching. "Sometimes they only get so many chances, no matter how much you love them." She reached for her napkin, unfolded it, and placed it on her lap. "If you don't mind, I'd rather not talk about my unfortunate experience with strays." Harry studied her, gave her a nod that said she didn't fool him, not one bit. That nod said she wasn't quite done with the stray who'd owned her heart and she knew it.

Harry made his way to their table three more times before the meals were served. *Let me know if you need anything. It sure is good to see you again.* And the last and most obvious attempt to let her dinner companion know Gina was a married woman. *Tell that husband of yours when he comes in again I've got a plate of calamari waiting for him...on the house.* A deep laugh followed by *And I won't even try to trick him into a side order of tripe.*

After the third comment about Gina and the reference to Ben, Pearson lifted his wine glass, swirled the contents around, and said in a casual manner, "Guess he wants to make sure I know about Ben."

Pearson didn't use the word *husband* when he referred to Ben but called him *that guy, Ben,* and once in a while he even said *fool.* Gina ignored the comments, didn't stop to consider what any of it meant. She didn't like games or trying to read between the lines. If a person had something to say, they should spit it out and be done. That's how it had always been with Ben—until the accident. Sometimes, it hadn't been necessary to say a word and they knew what the other meant...

"So, what do you think about Harry's brother and the whole secret family stuff? Pretty bizarre, isn't it?"

Gina fingered her wine glass, sucked in a quiet breath as she contemplated her answer. She didn't miss the judgmental tone in his voice or the way he said the word *bizarre* as though it were inconceivable—and anyone associated with or engaging in such activity was a horrible person. Gina used to think that way before she knew Christine and Harry, before she became close with Lily.... "It's not an ideal situation, but sometimes life happens."

"Life happens? I can't even conceive of such a situation." He leaned back against the booth, sipped his wine. "My parents have been married forty-one years, still go to the same church, raised three children, never had a fight."

Never had a fight? That was what seemed inconceivable. She'd once heard that when the fighting stopped, the troubles began because people in healthy relationships disagreed, they argued, sometimes they even raised their voices. Before the accident that turned them into strangers, she and Ben disagreed *and* argued, though *she* was the one who raised her voice while he remained silent until she finished her rant. Ben usually touched her shoulder and said in a gentle voice, *Get it all out so we can start to fix this.* He'd always been able to calm her, make her feel safe. "I think arguing is healthy in a relationship as long as it's not combative or demeaning." She sipped her wine, thought of the nights she and Ben drank wine on their deck, talked about the future and the plans they had. Sometimes she'd sit on his lap and he'd unbutton her shirt and...

"Vanessa and I never argued. When it's right, it's just right. I think it's all about finding that special person to share your life with and once that happens, you're set."

Why had she never noticed Pearson's close-mindedness before? Maybe because she'd been too absorbed hearing about his surgeries and the subsequent rehabilitative periods. But did he really believe if you found the right person to share your life, you wouldn't face challenges? She should keep her mouth shut, but she couldn't. "What happened when you and Vanessa disagreed? Would you just stay quiet?"

He shrugged, his blonde hair shimmering under the soft lights. "That's the thing. We never disagreed."

Gina scrunched her nose. "Pearson, you *never* disagreed? Not even on how to replace the toilet paper roll? What about brands of coffee? Whether to go out to dinner or stay in?" She and Ben disagreed about most of it, and they actually tried to strong-arm the other into changing their opinion. It usually didn't work, though sometimes it did, and it never mattered because it became a game—an amusing one they both looked forward to and enjoyed.

"What can I say? I'm an easy-going guy: likable, thoughtful, considerate. The perfect mate."

Something in those blue eyes bothered her. Maybe it was the way they narrowed and sparked when he said the word *mate*, or maybe it was the way he homed in on her lips.

"Lucky you. Can't say I've ever known any couple who agreed on everything." Even Nate and Christine disagreed. So did Cash and Tess. And Adam and Bree? Well, that was a whole other story. But the disagreements were healthy and respectful, and the couples were made for each other—just like she'd once believed she and Ben were made for each other.

"I was lucky, and I'd like to think when I find someone, she'll think she's lucky, too." His lips pulled into a slow smile.

"So, this is nice. The only thing that might make it nicer is if Harry Blacksworth didn't try to make me feel like there was another person sitting next to you."

"You mean my husband?"

Those lips flattened seconds before the smile corrected itself. "Right, that guy."

"There's no pretending he doesn't exist, because he does." *And if I have to admit the truth, he'll always live in my heart.*

"I understand that; trust me, I do. But at some point, he gets relegated to the past so you can move on."

"Move on? Move on to what? He's the father of my children and he won't be pushed into the past. Pearson, Ben and I are separated. We aren't divorced."

That blue gaze burrowed into her. "Yet."

It was that single word that made her look at Pearson Taylor in a different way. Did the man believe a few cafeteria lunches and chatting about rotator cuff and tennis elbow surgeries constituted a *relationship*? Well, he'd better readjust his thinking because Gina wasn't interested in anything but pure friendship, though after what she'd heard tonight, she'd pass on the friendship, too. She might be more comfortable with numbers and lists than trying to determine hidden meanings in a conversation, but the signal that he wanted a serious relationship with her was beacon-glaring bright. When Harry delivered the chicken Marsala and gnocchi in vodka sauce, she thanked him, told him she looked forward to meeting Cooper. Mention of his rescue dog brought a wide smile to his face and a soft *Everybody should have a dog.*

He hadn't taken four steps from the table before Pearson heaved a sigh that said *Disagree.* "Animals. I bet he lets that dog on the furniture. Can you imagine the hair? And the smell? Not in my house. No way."

Gina and Ben had talked about getting a dog but decided to wait until Ava was a little older. Neither had one growing up and thought a Labrador retriever would be good. Ben used to laugh and say *We'll rescue one like you rescued me.* Obviously, Pearson wasn't interested in a dog or anything that smelled or made a mess. He was very opinionated about it, and maybe those *opinions* were why he and his wife had never disagreed. She'd probably been tucked in a corner and told to remain quiet.

Pearson twirled a forkful of pasta, shook his head. "Dogs. Worse than cats."

"I like dogs. I'm thinking about getting one." *There, now do you think I'm a perfect mate?*

"You want a dog? Really?" The forkful of spaghetti unraveled, landed on his plate. "I never took you for a dog person."

"Oh, yes, I love dogs. I'm thinking about a Great Dane. So soft and gentle, good with kids, a little on the large side, but..." She let out a laugh, continued with her fabrication. "I'm also interested in an Irish wolfhound, or maybe a mastiff, but some say you can't go wrong with a Newfoundland."

Pearson set down his fork, stared at her. "Those dogs are bigger than you. Can you imagine how much they eat? Why would you want one of those?" He leaned toward her, held her gaze. "Gina, why would you want *any* dog?"

That was it. She was not going to sit here and listen to his opinions about people, dogs, or her husband. Gina removed the napkin from her lap, set it on the table, an indication that she was done with dinner... And if he were smart, he'd realized she was done with this conversation. "Why would I want a dog? Because dogs give us unconditional love, and nobody, not even humans, can do that."

THE DISASTROUS DINNER with Pearson Taylor couldn't end soon enough. Talk dwindled after her comment about dogs and unconditional love, and twenty minutes later, he pulled his luxury sedan into her driveway. Gina thanked him and rushed out of the car before good manners forced him to walk her to the door. That was a big *no thank you.* The man might know how to fix shoulders and elbows, but he had no idea how to navigate common courtesy or the use of kindness among strangers. Ugh. She'd seriously misread him.

When the doorbell rang, Gina hesitated. Had Pearson come to apologize for his behavior? Please no! He could apologize tomorrow, though she doubted the man thought he did anything wrong. What could he want? Gina sucked in a breath and opened the door. "Ben?" She took in the disheveled hair, the wild eyes, the paleness beneath his tan. "What's wrong?"

"Can I come in for a second?"

Something had happened. She stepped aside, let him enter. "Tell me what's wrong."

His voice turned hoarse. "Are you seeing that doctor?"

"What? Where did you hear that?" Someone must have seen them at Harry's Folly tonight and made a beeline to Ben. Who would have done it? If it were Harry, she'd be after him and not happy.

"Is it true?" He stuffed his hands in his coat pocket, stared at her as if the thought of her and Pearson together was too painful to consider. "Tell me, is it true?"

The hoarse voice reminded her of Cash's last birthday party when he and Ben had too much to drink. Gina pushed the memory away, homed in on Ben. "You don't get to ask those questions, Ben. Not anymore," she reminded him.

He ignored her, his blue eyes turning brighter. "It's true, isn't it? You've given up on us and moved on." The accusations swirled between them, coated in pain and disbelief. "You care about him."

The man did not deserve an answer, not after what he'd put her through. And if he were foolish enough to think she'd taken up with Pearson Taylor, then he didn't know her very well. "You have no right asking that question, and you know it. But what hurts me more is that you think I could just move on like you're a pair of shoes that grew too uncomfortable. I thought you knew me better than that, but maybe you don't." Anger seeped through her next words. "Or maybe you're using the same rationalization you did when you shut me out. Is it guilt that's bothering you?"

He eased his hands from his coat pocket, dragged them over his face. "It's every damn thing that happened between us. Every opportunity I missed, every pain I caused you, every minute I turned you away. The regret consumes me, and all I can see is what I lost." His voice cracked, split open. "Tell me I haven't lost you. Please, tell me there's still a chance."

She opened her mouth to admit the truth; no one could ever compare to the magic, the brightness that came from loving him, but the words stuck in her throat, held there by fear. He waited for the words that did not come, his expression a mix of pain, hope, and misery.

"I can't give up on us, Gina. All I have left is hope and I can't give up on that." He moved toward her, framed her face with those hands that knew every inch of her. "I love you. I will always love you," he whispered seconds before he took her mouth in a kiss filled with such gentleness, it made her lightheaded. She clutched his forearms for support, leaned toward him. Oh, but she had missed him, missed his touch, the taste of him, the—

Ben broke the kiss, pulled back. "I miss you so damn much." He tucked a lock of hair behind her ear, traced her jawline. "So damn much." Then he let his hand drop to his side and stepped away. "Good-night, Gina." One last look and he was gone, taking the warmth that had smothered her with him.

15

Ben lay on the bed at the Heart Sent, reading an article about composting. Apparently, there was green waste and brown waste and you had to have certain amounts of each for a successful composting bin. If he ever had a chance with Gina again, he thought she might like to dabble in composting. You could even get a mini-composter bin to hold the kitchen scraps until you dumped them in the big bin outside. The "mini" looked like a small garbage can with a charcoal filter to snuff out the smell. Now *that* was clever, and while Gina didn't like clutter on the counters, he didn't think she'd mind one of these. Huh. He flipped a page, read what you could throw in the kitchen composter: coffee grounds plus filters, veggie peelings, eggshells... Alex might like composting, too. It could be his own science project and it was good for the environment. Gina would like that idea, plus the compost would give her better soil for the flowers she loved so much.

There was a lot they could do together, but the way things were going, he might never get the chance. Maybe he'd blown it tonight when he kissed her. *Stupid, stupid, stupid.* What had he been thinking? Right. He hadn't been thinking. Emotion consumed him when Bree called him in an agitated state to deliver the news that she'd spotted Gina and this Pearson doctor guy at Harry's Folly. She'd tried to get the words out, but it was hard to understand their meaning with all of the *I cannot believe it* and *How could she do this?* and *Oh, goodness, this is so not good.* Ben might not be happy with Bree's husband right now, but the guy said in two sentences what Bree hadn't been able to say in ten. *Gina and the doctor are eating at Harry's Folly. The doctor's trying to get cozy.*

It was that last line that sent Ben to the house. *Trying to get cozy?* Was the guy at the house now? Sitting in Ben's recliner? Drinking his scotch? Kissing his wife? Doing more than kissing? It was a short drive to the house but by the time he got there, he was too worked up to think straight. When Gina opened the door, face flushed, eyes bright, so damn beautiful, he knew she could have any man she wanted.

And that's why he'd kissed her. *Because* he *wanted to be that man.* But that wasn't going to happen anytime soon. He considered all the ways he'd blown his chances and was up to number twelve when the knock on his bedroom door disrupted him. He glanced at his watch, slid off the bed. It was 10:20 p.m., long past Mimi's bedtime. Maybe she couldn't sleep, or maybe... He opened the door, curious to see why Mimi was still awake.

But the woman on the other side of the door wasn't Mimi. "Gina?"

"Hi, can we talk?"

"Uh, sure." He stepped aside to let her in, hesitated. "Where are the kids? Are they okay?"

"They're at Cash and Tess's tonight."

Probably so Gina could go to dinner with the doctor. Ben pushed back the jealousy that said his wife might have found his replacement and cleared his throat. "Do you want to talk downstairs? I can make you a cup of tea, or..."

She shook her head, avoided his gaze. "No, that's not necessary."

Ben eased the door closed, stuffed his hands in his pockets, and waited. He'd stay near the door, several feet from her so he didn't do something stupid again—like try to kiss her. He eyed his wife, noted the pale face, the furrowed brow, the frown. This was about that damn kiss. He blew out a sigh, cleared his throat. "I know why you're here, and I'm sorry. I have no excuse for what happened, but it won't happen again." *Not unless you want it to*...though the look on her face said *Don't count on it*.

Those dark eyes shimmered and when she spoke her voice was whisper-soft. "You mean the kiss?"

Had he imagined the breathiness in her words, the kind that used to saturate her speech when she was pleased, usually with him? Ben narrowed his gaze, tried to figure out if the sound were real or imagined, but with Gina, it was hard to tell. "Yeah. The kiss."

"I..." She licked her lips, opened her mouth to speak, closed it.

Gina at a loss for words? Hard to imagine, unless she were really ticked at him. Then it was more about holding the words inside until the exact moment when she'd blast him with an arsenal of them. But not being able to *find* the words? Nope. Not

Gina. Unless the words were too painful to speak. Ben moved toward her, stopped when he was a touch away. Had he pushed her too far? Made her realize she wanted to end the marriage for good? "Did you come here about a divorce?" There, he'd said it.

"No!" She reached out, touched his arm. "No, that's not why I came."

He blew out a breath as relief poured through him. *She hadn't come for a divorce!* Ben glanced at Gina's hand, resting on his bare arm. When he spoke, he kept his voice gentle. "Why are you here, Gina?"

"I...I... I want..." Her bottom lip quivered, her shoulders shook, and the tears fell, blocked out her answer. She swiped at her cheeks, but those damn tears kept coming. Ben opened his arms and she flung herself at his chest, wrapped her arms around his waist, clung to him.

"Hey, it's okay." He held her close, stroked her back, murmured soothing words like he used to when she was upset. She'd once told him he was the only person who could calm her, but he'd stopped believing that when he'd become the cause of the upsets. There could only be so many reasons she'd sought him out, and if it wasn't for a divorce, and it wasn't about the kiss, then what? "Is it the doctor guy? Do you and he...?"

"No," she mumbled against his T-shirt.

More relief shot through him, pierced a tiny hole in his heart where joy seeped out. "I know I shouldn't say this, but...I'm glad."

Gina eased back, her face smeared with tears and mascara smudges. "Oh, Ben," she whispered. "How could I look at another man when I compare them all to you?"

"Me?" Ben tightened his grip on her, tried to understand what she was saying.

"It's always been you, Ben." She sniffed, held his gaze as fresh tears spilled. "Only you."

The kiss came next as she leaned on tiptoe, laced her hands behind his neck, and pulled him closer. Hot, deep, consuming. Gina devoured his mouth, his senses...his heart. "I want you."

How many nights had he dreamed this? How many times had he hoped for one more chance with the only woman he'd ever loved? The need to make love to her burst through him, but he pushed it away. He didn't want to scare her; he would go slowly. He would show her patience and—

"I can't wait," she murmured into his ear, her voice a mix of need and impatience. "It's been too long."

"But..."

Gina stifled his words with another kiss, this one deeper, slower, more passionate. She became the aggressor as she unbuckled his belt, reached for his zipper...led him to the bed. It was Gina who crawled on top of him, half-clothed minus the scrap of underwear she'd discarded seconds before she eased onto his sex with a satisfied moan. *"Oh, yes."* There was no talking after that except for *Again* and *More* and twice there'd been a *Please*, though later he'd wonder if the *please* meant *again, more,* or *both.* Their lovemaking had been intense, and surreal as Gina worked his body in ways that told him he'd been a fool to think he'd disappoint her in bed.

They made love twice and Ben thought about a third time, but exhaustion won out. He pulled Gina against, him, her head resting on his chest, arm flung around his waist. Joy. Peace. Hope. As he drifted to sleep, he knew all of these, and in the morning, they would speak of one more: love.

But when morning came, Gina was gone.

Ben rolled over, stared at the spot where she'd slept last night. Visions of their lovemaking shot through him, the hope she'd planted in his heart, the joy. This morning he'd planned to talk about the love he had for her, the love that lived in his soul. And then she'd admit the same and they could start rebuilding their life together, better and stronger than ever. He'd move back home, and they'd be a family again, a real family, and nothing would ever come between them again.

That's why she'd come last night...to show him just how much she wanted them to work. Except, why would she duck out this morning before they had a chance to talk about last night? *Oh, yes, again* and *more* didn't qualify as talking. They were more like exclamation points at the end of a fantastic dinner. Ben sat on the edge of the bed, took in the boxer shorts on the floor several feet away. His jeans were closer, next to his T-shirt. Where were his socks? Hell, if he could remember how he'd gotten out of them.

So... What now? What were the chances Gina was fixing them breakfast in Mimi's kitchen? Okay, how about just coffee? He homed in on the pillow next to his. Not a single dark hair, nothing but a slight indentation. A burn in the pit of his belly started when he considered the reason for her quick exit.

It hadn't been about getting back together. It hadn't even been about finding joy or hope and forget about love. Nope, maybe the real reason she'd come last night was the most obvious: it was all about the sex.

~

GINA COULDN'T AVOID her husband any longer. She'd thought

he'd call her the second he woke and found her gone, but he hadn't. Nor had he shown up at the house yesterday looking for answers; another shocker. She'd have sworn he'd demand to know why she'd taken off, and worse, why she'd shown up in the first place.

So, why *had* she shown up at the Heart Sent the other night? She'd told herself it had nothing to do with the kiss that stole her logic and made her crave more—much more, but that was such a lie. She'd wanted Ben's touch, his body covering hers, mouth trailing kisses along the sensitive area of her neck, her breasts... It had been so long... She'd wanted to feel that pure pleasure again, all of it. Of course, she couldn't admit *that*, not with words, but it hadn't been necessary because Ben had always known what she needed, what she wanted, and he'd certainly known the other night.

But then early morning had come, and she'd awakened to his naked body next to hers, his arm flung around her middle —strong, possessive, caring. Panic and the memory of how good they were together forced her from his bed. Hurt and betrayal snuffed out the closeness she'd felt, replaced it with the reminder that life could not be lived in the bedroom.

Could she and Ben have a life together again, one built on trust, love, and commitment? She didn't know and that's why she'd avoided him. *But why was he avoiding her?* Gina got her answer the next afternoon when Ben stopped by to deliver yogurt, applesauce, and bananas for the kids. When she greeted him, those blue eyes stared at her a second too long, slid from her lips to the V-neck top, settled on the necklace dangling at the hollow of her throat before inching back to her eyes.

"Hello, Gina."

That voice had the ability to make her forget why they

shouldn't be together. "Hello, Ben." She turned, pointed toward the kitchen, away from that intense gaze that saw too much. "You can bring the groceries in here."

"Sure." He followed her, set the bag on the kitchen table, began to remove the yogurt.

Such strong hands... She let out a soft sigh, kept her gaze on those hands.

"Ahem."

Gina shot a glance at her husband, blushed at the narrowed gaze. He'd caught her staring and no doubt from the smokiness of those blue eyes, he knew she was thinking about the other night. How could she *not* think about it? She opened the fridge, placed six yogurts on the top right shelf, closed the door. "Guess we should talk about the other night."

"Guess so."

He was not going to make this easy on her. "I...had a nice time," she ventured.

"Nice? Hmm." He leaned against the counter, crossed his arms over his chest, and studied her. "I would have used another term, but maybe that's why you left." Pause, a raised brow. "Because it was only *nice*."

Her attempt at laughter splattered between them. This was *not* going well. Gina licked her lips, tucked a lock of hair behind her ear. "You know what I mean."

"No, actually, I don't."

A half smile and a soft "Better than nice."

"Ah."

Why was he not smiling? Why were the brackets around his mouth an inch deep, his lips pulled into a frown? She tried again. "Really. A lot better."

He nodded, shrugged. "Thanks. I try."

"So..."

"Yes?"

There was so much uncertainty between them, but one area that had never been anything but perfect was the physical part. Maybe they could start there and see where it took them? Yes, maybe that's what they should do. She moved toward him, tried again for a smile. "I'm sorry I left the other night, but I had to think." The words tumbled out. "There are certain areas of our relationship that have always been..."

His voice dipped, swirled over her like a caress. "Perfect?"

"Yes. Perfect." He understood what she meant, and from the softening of those brackets, he agreed. Maybe he'd agree to the rest. "We could start from there, couldn't we?"

"Meaning?"

The brackets appeared again, deeper than before. "Meaning, why not continue with the part that works?" Had the muscles in his jaw twitched just now? Did he not like that idea? What man would turn down an offer of sex without expectations? Gina should have known Ben Reed wasn't just any man; he was her husband and he wasn't settling for less. His next words proved it.

"You want me for the sex?"

Why did he have to sound so cold about it? Couldn't they consider it unspoken communication and go from there? Gina cleared her throat, pushed out an explanation that made sense to her if she removed their history, emotion, and the fact that he was her husband. "It could be a starting point."

That made him laugh. "A starting point? To what? More sex?"

"No..." Maybe if they started with the physical part of

their relationship, they could work up to the talking, the sharing, the trusting...

His expression shifted from disbelief to hurt. "Look, I want the whole package, not just the bedroom, and I can't believe you'd be okay with that."

"But—"

"Some guys might think it's a great deal. Not this guy. I want the wife that goes with it."

Gina bit her bottom lip. "I'm not sure I can give you that." There, she'd said it.

"I figured that out when you left my bed."

"Ben—"

"Save it, Gina. I get it. I hurt you, and I should feel the pain, but I'm starting to think you're never going to let that go. If that's true, just tell me. Don't string me along and make me believe we've got a shot when we don't. Can you do that?"

"I need more time."

He eyed her. "I can't undo what happened, but I'm trying to show you how much I care. I love you, Gina, but maybe that's not enough."

16

Ben sipped his coffee, flipped through the morning report on his desk. Noise disturbance at 2:00 a.m., missing lawn furniture, lost dog... The last one caught his eye. *Lost dog reported at 10:14 p.m. last night by Harry Blacksworth.*

Harry? Was this the rescue dog everybody in town said lived like a prince? Wild salmon and pureed sweet potatoes? Four orthopedic beds? Filtered water? His own exercise and agility training course in the backyard? That sounded like Harry Blacksworth; the guy's heart was bigger than his common sense. Ben picked up the phone, punched out the phone number on the report.

"Hello?"

"Harry? Ben Reed. I'm calling to see if your dog showed up yet."

"Nope. Not yet."

The man's voice was a mix of pure misery and hopelessness. "Okay, why don't you tell me where you've checked and if you have any idea where he might have gone."

A loud sigh spread through the phone. "I never let Cooper out the front door unless he's on his leash. I swear I don't." More misery poured through the lines. "But Lizzie left her sneakers on the front lawn—two pairs of them—said Lily Desantro told her they could turn colors under the stars and she wanted them to turn pink. My wife wasn't happy about that, so I went after them. Cooper snuck out behind me and next thing I knew, he was gone." He cleared his throat twice. "Can you help me find him? I've been everywhere I can think of and I don't know where else to look."

Ben was still supposed to be on desk duty, but who would know if he slipped out for an hour to look for Harry's dog? Rudy wasn't due in until after lunch, and the Blacksworths were technically friends... He'd go with the helping-out-a-friend story if Rudy found out.

"Give me a few minutes, and I'll swing by your house."

"Thanks, Ben. I owe you."

"Just part of the job."

Fifty minutes later Ben wasn't so sure it was *just part of the job*. Walking through muddy trails near Nate's house because Harry thought his dog might migrate to a wooded area? Calling the dog's name until he grew hoarse? Whistling? Switching out Cooper's name for *Come here, Big Guy*? Ben did it all, and Harry Blacksworth was right beside him, but it didn't matter, because the dog wasn't there.

After an hour of yelling and tramping over the wet ground, Ben turned to Harry. The guy wasn't going to want to hear it, but maybe the dog *wasn't* coming back. Maybe he'd decided it was time to run free. Why stay in a mansion when he could roam the streets, eat road kill, sleep on wet dirt? No rules, no commands, nothing but his own brain telling him what he did and didn't want to do.

Damn, but the dog sounded a lot like Ben after the injury, when he thought he could do whatever he wanted, and no one could control him, especially his wife. Look how that had turned out. All he had left was a wife who wanted the sex part of the relationship without the rest of it. Nice. Ben pushed thoughts of Gina's proposal to the back of his brain where he hoped he could forget about it for longer than a minute. "Got any other ideas, Harry?"

The poor guy shook his head, shoved his hands in his jacket pockets, and said in a pitiful voice, "Nope. I'm having flyers made, but..." His blue eyes glistened with what looked a lot like tears. "How's my boy going to find his way back home?" Another shake of his head, and a curse word. "Maybe I shouldn't have been so tough on him. Would it have been a big deal if he jumped on one of the couches? So what if he scratched the leather?" Big sigh, more cursing. "That's what leather repair companies are for, right?" He didn't wait for Ben's response, but plowed on, adding curses and head shakes with each comment. "Bet he wanted a steak every now and again, too. I mean, who can live on salmon and sweet potatoes, even if they're ground and pureed? I wouldn't want to, would you?"

Ben rubbed his jaw. "No, can't say I would."

"Exactly, but my wife said the dog needed rules. She said it's all about consistency and making them feel safe. Hell, I bet Cooper couldn't wait to bolt so he could taste meat, even if it was raw and mashed from tire tracks."

That was an interesting visual. Ben scanned the area ahead of them: nothing but more trees and a dirt trail. He hated to admit it, but it looked like Cooper might be gone for good. "Harry, I'm happy to help you, but I don't know where else to look, and I should get back to work."

Harry Blacksworth, the transplanted gazillionaire Chicagoan with one of the biggest hearts in Magdalena, nodded, shoulders slumped. "I know. Appreciate it, Ben. Guess it wasn't meant to be." He took one last look toward the trail ahead, let out a pathetic groan. "Might as well head back. No sense dragging this out any longer. I'm gonna have to tell the kids, and I am not looking forward to that. Greta says being a parent means you're there for the good *and* bad times. I know she's right, but I hate disappointing them."

"I know, but I think it's about helping them through the disappointment that counts. Just having them know you're there and not giving up." He wasn't giving up on being a father, no matter how things ended between him and Gina. There might have been a period after the accident where he'd failed at the job, but he vowed that would not happen again. He wanted the same opportunity to be a husband again, but adults, especially his wife, were not as forgiving as children.

"I bet you're a good dad, Ben." Harry trudged along the path, sloshing mud on his dress trousers and high-end hiking boots. "Greta says it's all about just showing up, that it doesn't matter if you screw up, just show up." He let out a soft laugh. "I think she's right, but then she usually is." He slid Ben a look. "Ever realize how much our women know about life?" When Ben nodded, Harry let out another laugh, scratched his head. "Do you think it's because men are idiots who can't see the answers when they're sitting on top of us, or are women just better at ferreting out the truth?"

Now there was a question. Ben fixed his gaze on the clearing ahead where he'd parked the police cruiser. "I'd say both."

"So would I." Pause, and then "So, you and Gina..."

"Right." No need to fill in the blanks because Ben guessed

Harry figured out the Reeds still weren't together and might not end up together either. At least the guy didn't put sound to it, didn't call Ben out on his monumental screw-up, or his association with Emma Hale. At least there was that small consolation when most of the town was still shooting him the evil eye for being such a jerk. What would they think if they knew he wanted to make his marriage work, but his wife was only interested in conjugal visits?

When they reached the clearing where the police cruiser sat, Harry stomped his boots, took one last look around the area before he opened the door and slid into the front seat. "You'll be okay, Ben. You're a good guy, but our women are tough." He latched his seatbelt, yawned. "Greta and Gina are no-nonsense types who won't let us get away with squat. It's damn admirable but it can be a pain when you're looking for a little wiggle room." He sighed, glanced out the window. "Those two don't know the meaning of the terms *cutting slack* or *going easy*. Nope, they're going to make us own up to our words or eat them." He slid Ben a look. "I've had to eat mine a few times, and it's been damn uncomfortable, especially when I knew she was dead on."

"That sounds about right." He bet Greta Blacksworth hadn't told *her* husband she wanted sex without the relationship.

"Hang in there. Don't give in to a sap like that doctor. Straight-laced pain in the ass." He scratched his jaw, muttered, "Who doesn't like dogs?"

Ben guessed Harry was talking about Pearson Taylor. The guy sounded full of himself and not someone Gina would be interested in, on a professional or personal level. But who knew? *Damn it, who knew anything anymore?*

When they reached the Blacksworth mansion, Ben pulled

in the driveway and seconds later the door burst open and out came Greta, AJ, Lizzie...and Cooper. Harry let out a shout that could reach Renova and almost jumped out of the car. "It's him! Ben, did you see? It's Cooper!"

"I see that, Harry." Ben pulled the cruiser to a stop, shut it off, and stepped out.

"Cooper! Come here, boy!" Harry scrambled up the driveway, arms wide, jacket flapping, a man on a mission to reunite with his family.

Ben took it all in: the shouts of joy as Harry hugged his rescue dog, smacked a kiss on his wife's mouth, bearhugged each child. Harry Blacksworth might have been a stray, but he'd found his pack and he wasn't letting go. Ever.

"He found his way back, Harry." Greta's eyes shone bright, her voice trembled. "Wet and dirty, with brambles on his coat. We bathed and fed him, tucked him in his bed. I tried to call, but you left your phone on the couch." She raised a brow. "Lizzie said you were letting her play games on it again." The sheepish look he gave her said Lizzie was correct. "Harry." Greta's soft voice mixed with her accent held a hint of scolding. "We talked about this. Rules, remember? And consistency, that's how this works."

He nodded, stroked her cheek. "I'll do better, Greta. Don't give up on my sorry butt just yet."

The smile she gave him lit up her face. "Never, Harry. No matter what." The raised brow came next. "But you may need a few adjustments."

MEN MADE the mistake of believing they'd know how to spot a manipulator, especially one bent on doing them harm, but when the compliments and the fluff talk started, it was game over. These fools got so turned around and lapped up the sugar crap so fast, they didn't realize it was loaded with enough poison to destroy their lives, their marriages, their happiness. By the time they did, it was too damn late: damage done, marriage over, manipulation complete. And for what? BS words that did nothing but pump up a guy's fat head? Harry rubbed his jaw, studied the manipulator in the corner, blew out a slow breath. Emma Hale had done damage, but maybe there was still hope for the poor sucker she'd reeled in and the woman he'd hurt.

Did men really fall for crap like *You're incredible, such a great guy...the best... I've never met a man like you... Don't let anybody tell you what you can and can't do... You're a king, but you already know that, don't you? Live your life now...don't regret what you didn't do...*

He could hear it all now. Crap and more crap, all stuffed into an ego booster that some down-on-his-luck guy would slurp up in two seconds and then ask for more. Until he opened his eyes one day and saw the truth: he'd been an idiot and he'd been played. Harry could hold classes on how to spot a manipulator because the guys in this town were getting blindsided. It had happened to Cash when the you're-a-baby-daddy woman came to town with a kid and a story that was pure BS. But the guy couldn't see past anything but the boy who looked like him and the I'm-dying sob story. Lies. Clever ones, and the woman had been a pro, but still... Harry would have spotted her for what she was because he'd seen that type before. That's how he knew how to handle the woman when it came time to settle the deal; money still talked, especially to *those* people.

But this new one wasn't about money. She'd come at Ben

Reed sideways, all pure and innocent, an angel from his hometown who vowed to help him recover. Who wouldn't fall for that story, especially when she'd been hired by the guy's wife? Poor sap had been so tied up in his own pity-party that he'd missed the signals that said *I want you and I'm going to have you.* Ben Reed had a lot going for him and was an all-around good guy who loved his wife and kids, but that damn fall from the ladder really screwed him up, made him angry, pissed off, and hell, probably depressed.

Not good, but it sure had proved fertile hunting ground for a woman like Emma Hale.

She'd taken advantage of it, and he'd never seen it coming until it was too late.

Why did men think the innocent-looking ones weren't as dangerous as the red-lipped seducers?

When this was all over and Ben and Gina were back together—and he damn well hoped they would be—maybe he'd hold a meeting at the restaurant for the men in this town, serve them their favorite dishes, open a few bottles of wine, and give a talk called *Don't get played by a player.* Yeah, he liked the sound of that.

Harry adjusted his tie and made his way toward Emma Hale's booth. "So, you're the physical therapist everybody's talking about." Pretty thing, slender like a willow, a real looker in a fresh-faced way: pure, clean, the take-home-to-mother kind. Looks didn't always tell the whole story.

She pinched her lips and those tiny nostrils flared like she didn't care for the comment or the reference. "Yes, and you must be Harry Blacksworth. I've heard a lot about you."

"No doubt you have." He laughed, slid into the booth opposite her, and laid his hands flat on the table. "I have a habit of saying whatever lands in my head. My wife's trying to teach me, but I guess I don't have any manners when it comes to that." He tossed her a look, threw in a smile. "Know what I mean? Sometimes you gotta say what's on your mind and to hell with people's feelings."

The brows came together, the lips pinched more, but somehow the words slid out. "I believe in honesty, but it can be cruel."

Honesty? The woman didn't know the meaning of that word, not if the tales he'd heard were true. "Sure. I learned fast that honesty's what makes a marriage work." He threw her another smile. "Ever been married? You know, the whole vows thing."

She shook her head. "No."

He thrummed his fingers on the white tablecloth. "This married business is damn tough. It's a crapshoot, and sometimes the deck's stacked. But if you get a good one, you hang on, no matter what. Still doesn't make it easy and it doesn't mean there aren't times when you're so ticked at that other person you want to freeze them out of the room. But you don't, because when everything's laid out on the table, they're the one who'll stand by your side and walk through hell with you."

The woman lifted her slender shoulders, studied him. "So I've heard. However, there are instances when the battle *becomes* the marriage. When that happens, it's time to reconsider the agreements."

Harry narrowed his gaze on her, tried to peck around the words and their meaning. "Agreements? Oh, you mean the marriage?"

"Yes, the marriage."

"Maybe, but if there's one thing I learned since I settled down, it's that every marriage has its troubles, and every husband and wife do battle. If they don't, if there's no arguing, then the war's already lost. But you know what the real problem is? When some third party comes waltzing in, offering solutions she knows nothing about to a situation she knows nothing about, brainwashing the husband to believe he doesn't have to follow rules because there are none." He rubbed his jaw, zinged her with his next words. "But it's all BS because there are *always* rules."

Those full lips thinned. "Maybe there shouldn't be."

"Huh. I'm more of a rule breaker than a rule maker, but if you don't have any, well, that's a downward slide to chaos. The third party doesn't care about that when she's trying to convince the guy *she* knows what he needs—" Harry paused, rubbed his jaw "—and it isn't the wife and kids or the swing set in the backyard. She has no idea what it's like to be in the trenches. She's never been in them, doesn't know about the joy, the sadness, the damn loss. Never pictured the guy on the couch with a fever and the flu, or leaving his underwear on the floor, or throwing up and missing the toilet. Nope, no shining light there because she doesn't think it exists, just like he doesn't think she'd be a nagger telling him what he should and shouldn't do. That's the real crime because it's a fairy tale, and we both know the minute the third party convinces him there are no rules, she's got him."

Oh, she didn't like that. Those dark eyes simmered, the slender jaw twitched. "If the marriage is already over or if there's a crack in it, then what's the harm?"

Harry wanted to jump out of the booth and kick her skinny butt from the restaurant. "You're talking about lives here: husbands and wives, children. You don't go butting in where you don't belong. Or do you think you *do* belong?"

"If we're talking about Ben Reed, and it's obvious we are,

he's a big boy who can make his own decisions. And like I said to anyone bold enough to confront me, including Gina, if the marriage is solid and the love is true, nothing will break the relationship."

"You leave the Reeds alone. They belong together, and Gina's first mistake was trusting you to help her husband. All you wanted to do was lock your sights on your next prey, and Ben was vulnerable." He gripped the edge of the table, leaned close, spat out, "You took advantage of him, but you better leave him alone."

"Nobody can take advantage of another person unless they permit it." She removed the napkin from her lap, placed it on the table, and slid out of the booth. "You might consider adding a few heart-healthy options to your list." She paused, raised a slender brow. "It's the responsible thing to do, don't you think?" Before he could tell her what to do with her responsible comments, she tossed him a smile that was about as real as the muffins in Lizzie's tea set and left.

17

Twenty-four weeks after the accident

Ben had taken Alex and Ava to Mimi Pendergrass's so Alex could see the train set that once belonged to Mimi's son. The boy had a fascination with trains and when Mimi learned about this, she dug out the train set from the attic and invited Alex to see it. Gina couldn't imagine how difficult it must be for Mimi to share her dead son's gift with another child. Did the wounds open every time she looked at it? Did the pain ever lessen? How could it? A child was a part of you: your breath, your life, your hope.

Gina thought of Alex and Ava, the children she never dreamed would one day be hers. Such love and hope, such joy. Years ago, she'd not believed she would ever have a husband *or* children, but there'd been a pocket of years when destiny had brought her Ben Reed and fate had shown her what true happiness was. What boundless love could do... What family meant. Now, family meant a mother, two children, and a father who lived in a different house.

"Gina? What's wrong?"

Lily Desantro studied her from behind thick glasses, the young girl's blue gaze intense. Gina forced a smile, shifted her voice to erase the sadness from it. "Just tired, I guess. And I miss the kids."

Lily nodded, dark curls bouncing. "And you miss Ben, too." She paused, tilted her head to the side. "Don't you?"

There was a question inside a million questions. Yes, she missed him, but the man who dropped off the kids, the one who spoke less than ten sentences and did it with a serious face and stingy smiles? She didn't know him. She should never have slept with Ben before she knew if she could recommit to their marriage, and she definitely should not have proposed a physical relationship—minus the relationship part. Why had she done that? *What was wrong with her?*

"So, do you miss him?"

"I do miss him." There was truth in those words, but sometimes the truth wasn't enough.

"He misses you, too."

Lily had come to help Gina plant petunias, geraniums, and impatiens, some in beds, some in pots. And then there were the seeds they'd harvested last fall: cosmos, zinnias, and alyssum. Lily had been after her mother to let her help Gina with the flowers because as she said, Gina had too much work with two kids, a job, and a husband who didn't live there. Usually Gina would refuse the help because letting anyone too close to her home might reveal the sadness lurking between the walls, seeping through the landscape. But she was already weeks behind with planting and Lily was special; she didn't judge, though she did observe. A lot.

When Gina didn't respond to Lily's comment about Ben missing her, Lily went on. "He's sad. His lips don't smile too much anymore unless he's talking to Alex or Ava. When I asked him why he didn't smile, he said it was because he didn't know if he would ever see sunshine again." She wrinkled her nose, tilted her head to one side. "Why would he say that? The sun's out now, and it was out that day, too."

Why *would* he say that? "I don't know, Lily. Sometimes people say one thing and mean something else." Like *I'll love you forever* when what they really mean is *I'll love you until things get difficult.*

Lily knelt on the ground next to a tray of petunias, held out her hands as Gina removed three plants from their container. Her lips pulled into a slow smile. "I think *you're* the sunshine," Lily said. "Because when Ben talks about you, his eyes sparkle, and his voice gets all soft like when he talks to Ava. He doesn't have a frowny face like most times." She squinted. "Are you his sunshine?"

He'd once told her she was the sunshine in his world, the one person who made things right and brought light and beauty into his life, filled his heart… "I don't know."

"Well, Nate says Ben has a lot to figure out and he said there wouldn't be so many problems if Ben had used the right head. What does he mean by that? A person only has one head. Everybody knows that." *Giggle, giggle, giggle.* "We don't have other heads."

Typical Nate. Gina bet Ben hadn't liked that, and Lily's next words told her she was right.

"Ben said Nate better be quiet because he was no angel." *Giggle, giggle, giggle.* "Nate's not an angel. And then Cash said something about sleeping in the wrong bed and not sleeping in the right bed, and it got too confusing because I don't know whose bed they were talking about."

Yes, whose bed *were* they talking about?

"Maybe they were talking about your bed, Gina."

Gina coughed, darted a glance at Lily. "What? Why would you say that?"

Lily sat back on her heels, pushed up her glasses. "Because Cash said this never would have happened if Ben stayed in the right bed. I think that's what he said. He said, the hospital bed was an excuse. Then Nate laughed and said something I couldn't hear. Ben said bad words, so I can't repeat them, but he told Cash to be quiet or he was going to make him be quiet." Her voice turned soft, worried. "Do you think Ben wanted to punch Cash? I hope not because Cash is so handsome, and I would never want him to get hurt."

The whole town knew about Lily Desantro's crush on Daniel Casherdon. "I'm sure Cash could take care of himself, but I don't think Nate would let that happen."

She nodded as if considering how her big brother would not let this happen. "Nate might give them a frowny face and talk real deep like he does when he's not happy, and then they would have to stop." She shrugged, turned back to the bucket of dirt by her side. When she spoke, her voice wobbled. "You aren't going to get a divorce, are you?"

What to say to that? *I don't know? I don't want to, but I don't know what's going to happen?* Gina removed a glove, placed a hand on Lily's shoulder and said in a gentle voice, "These are married people problems, Lily. Not ones you should worry about."

The girl sniffed, swiped at her cheek, smeared dirt there. "But I do worry about them. Ben loves you and you love Ben, and if you get a divorce Ben will never get his sunshine because he'll live in the dark forever." Her voice drifted, quivered with sadness. "He'll never get his sunshine again. You can't let that happen, Gina. You have to show him that you don't want him to stay at Mimi's. Tell him to come back and live in this house with you and Alex and Ava." She held Gina's gaze, sniffed again. "Don't let him go. He needs you." Lily nodded, her next words filled with wisdom and conviction. "And you need him, too."

~

NATALIE COULD NOT SIT by and watch her cousin's life fall apart. She owed it to Gina and one way or the other, she would see Ben and Gina together again. *No matter what it took.* Mimi had provided guidance and a few suggestions that included a twist in Natalie's attempts to get Emma Hale to do the right thing and leave the Reeds alone. Mimi said it was about finding and appealing to the woman's true weakness.

It was worth a try.

When Emma visited Natalie late one afternoon for a manicure, the woman appeared quieter than usual. This was the perfect opportunity to investigate. "What's wrong, Emma? You don't seem your usual happy self."

The woman shook her blonde head, let out a long sigh. "I'm not happy. In fact, I'm sad."

Yes, Natalie bet Emma was sad that her play for Gina's husband hadn't worked out the way she'd hoped. The rumors about town said Ben loved his wife and wanted to be done with the separation. "Does this have to do with Ben Reed?" *Tell me the truth, Emma. Because I already know it does.*

"Maybe." Those dark eyes turned bright. "Why can't men be who they say they are and do what they say they want to do? Is it all pretend? Do they just tell you they want a different life to make themselves feel big, when all they really want is a different version of that same life?"

"If you're talking about Ben, he needed help getting through a rough time, but he wasn't looking for a new life, and he certainly didn't want another wife. He only wanted Gina, the wife he had, but fear and insecurity held him back and made him question himself and his ability to be the husband he wanted to be. You gave him that hope back, and the strength to admit how much he wanted his wife *and* his marriage." Natalie held Emma's gaze, said in a voice filled with conviction, "Thank you for doing that, but please don't let misguided gratitude look like anything else."

A tear fell, slipped along Emma's cheeks to her chin. "You mean don't mistake it for love?"

Natalie nodded. "Exactly. I've known a lot of men and I can always tell the ones who're committed to their women and their marriage, and Ben Reed's committed to his."

"Doesn't he want a chance to find something better, maybe find someone who doesn't try to control him?"

The quiver in her voice told Natalie she wanted to be that person, thought Ben might want it, too. "No, when men like Ben fall in love, it's for keeps. They don't want do-overs or free falls of excitement or a promise of opportunity to live wide-open. They want the person they love and the life they love—it's called family. That's what makes them so enticing. Women like you and the me I used to be crave that. Oh, we say we'll let them do whatever they want, but what we don't say is that we're after the same love and commitment they gave their woman. Why wouldn't we want it? It's pure, honest, eternal." Natalie blinked, blinked again when she thought of the pain she'd caused Nate and Christine

Desantro. "But those men will never be ours and we have to realize that and let them go."

Emma sniffed. "I watched my mother reinvent herself dozens of times. Whatever the latest man wanted, she gave him. I hated it, vowed never to be like her. I became a physical therapist to heal bodies, but then I realized too many times the heart and soul were left untended and suffered for it. I knew I could take away that pain, help the healing, and I committed to doing that." Another sniff. "I became what patients needed me to be to heal them." Doubt clouded her expression. "Was it so wrong to make them believe they could have more: a new life, a renewed purpose, a partner who would not badger or judge? It healed them, Natalie. Was that so wrong?"

What to say to that? There'd been a time when Natalie believed she could and should be Nate's one-and-only, and when that didn't happen, she chose self-destruction by sleeping around, lying, and trying to destroy Nate's marriage. What Emma Hale had done to the Reeds and, no doubt, other couples, was no worse than what Natalie had done. But people could change if they opened their eyes and believed they deserved better. It had been a hard road for Natalie and some days she still didn't think she had a right to be this happy, but she wasn't giving it up. She was, however, going to take every opportunity to show the Good Lord and this town how grateful she was for a second chance. And right now, that meant helping Ben and Gina Reed and getting Emma Hale out of Magdalena.

"Natalie?" Emma reached out, touched her hand. "Was I wrong to give them what they needed?"

"You were wrong to create a fantasy that let them believe that's what they needed. This isn't about Ben or any other male patient you've fallen for...this is about *you*, Emma, and how you don't think you're enough and have to reinvent yourself for a guy." Natalie's voice spilled regret. "You've got to stop. It will destroy you and you're worth more than that."

Emma sniffed, dipped her head. "But I love Ben, love him so much it hurts my soul."

Did she even know what love meant? Did she know who Ben Reed really was? Natalie didn't think so, because if Emma did, she wouldn't try to steal him away by offering a life without Gina and the family he loved. "If you love him, then you must let him go to be with the one woman who owns his heart, the one who will always own his heart." Natalie leaned forward, whispered, "Gina. It's always been Gina. Please, give Ben the purest gift of your love you can. Leave him alone and let him be with Gina."

"You don't think there's any chance for us?"

She sounded pitiful and full of misery. Natalie remembered that feeling, but these days, she remembered the joy of loving her husband and son. "No chance. You've got to find your own happiness, Emma. Not with a guy, because if it's meant to be, that will come later—after you've worked on your own issues. Trust me, you *will* find joy, peace, and contentment." She paused, worked up a smile. "Then you'll be ready for a real relationship, not one headed for disaster because the guy's married or he's a patient. No more personal relationships with patients, Emma. That's a huge no. I'm talking about meeting an everyday person who's honest and decent, who will want to know the real Emma Hale, not the pretend one."

A glimmer of what looked an awful lot like hope sparked in Emma's dark eyes. "Okay." And then, "Thank you, Natalie. You've made me see things about myself I didn't want to see."

Another glimmer and this time, the hope shone through the misery. "Thank you."

"You're welcome. Now, I have one more question that you've been dodging since we first met. What brought you to Magdalena? We're a dot on the map, a pinpoint actually."

A pause, followed by a soft "That's easy."

And then she told Natalie about the woman in her yoga class named Paige whose cousin had moved to Magdalena, settled down, and found his own slice of happiness. Of course, that man was Ben.

Three days later, news of Emma Hale's departure from Magdalena spilled through town, fast, hard, and with such force it made people ask all sorts of questions and draw several conclusions, some right, some not.

Why did she leave?

Where did she go?

I heard she headed to Utah to take care of an injured skier. Broken leg, broken pelvis...bad...

No, she went back to Philly, didn't she?

That's not what I heard. I heard Gina booted her out of town.

My sources say Ben Reed booted her out, told her to stay away from the woman he loved...

Whisper, whisper, whisper.

She's no angel, not after a stunt like that...

Whoever heard of a woman trying to heal a man and steal him away from his wife...

Emma Hale, a she-devil with a halo...

She might have possessed the gift of healing, but she also had the ability to rip a person's soul apart, destroying his family...

Ben Reed has a lot of explaining to do... A lot forgiveness to ask for...

Gina Reed's the real angel.

If she takes Ben back, he better get down on his good knee and beg her forgiveness.

Gina Reed...Angel...Woman of power...

A true angel indeed.

~

DANIEL CASHERDON BELIEVED a man's integrity could be measured by his loyalty to family and friends. He'd vowed that if his family or friends were ever at risk, he'd take care of the threat. He never elaborated on what he'd do or how he'd do it, but with Cash, some things were best left unsaid. Gina had appreciated the comments and been comforted that he'd considered Ben one of those friends—maybe his best friend.

And it was loyalty that made him screech up Gina's driveway one afternoon, jump out of his truck, and stalk toward her, hands balled into fists, mouth a slash of anger. "Damn it, Gina, how could you?"

"Cash? What's wrong?" The man might have settled down with a family, two kids, and a dog, but sometimes the same old hothead he used to be still surfaced—like now.

"Ben. I swear, Gina, if you don't stop this, you are going to end up all alone."

She stiffened, squared her shoulders, and glared at him. "I have no idea what you're talking about. What did I do to Ben?" Had her husband told Cash about her suggestion to sleep together minus the relationship part? She forced herself to remain calm. *Would Ben do that?*

"He's done everything to gain your forgiveness and get another chance, but it's not enough for you, is it? You want to neuter him, and this is how you plan to do it." Those whiskey-colored eyes burned into her. "Can't you see you're tearing him apart?"

Maybe Ben *had* told Cash about the proposal. Still, Cash would have to spell it out before she'd admit it. "What do you think I did?"

He let out a laugh, harsh, cold. "That's a good one. As if you didn't know. He's selling the motorcycle."

"What?" *Selling his motorcycle?*

"See what desperation will do? Why, Gina?" He scowled. "Do you know what that bike means to him?"

"Of course, I do. It means freedom and stands for everything he left behind." There, she'd said it.

Cash shook his head, blew out his disgust. "You have no idea what the hell you're talking about. This isn't about freedom. This bike isn't about living in the past." He slashed a hand in the air, spat out, "This is about honoring a friend."

"What friend?" Ben had never mentioned a friend as the reason he kept the motorcycle.

Cash eyed her. "So, he never told you about Vince."

Gina shook her head. "No, who's Vince?"

"He was a fellow marine; he and Ben rode bikes together." He hesitated as though he weren't sure how much to tell her. "Maybe you should ask Ben."

"I'm asking you. Obviously, you think I should know." She narrowed her gaze on him. "And why did you say Vince *was* a friend? What happened to him?"

Cash frowned. "Vince was diagnosed with bone cancer and had to have his leg amputated below the knee. That was the end of the riding." Emotion smothered his words. "The cancer spread, and he didn't make it. That's when Ben vowed to ride for Vince."

Sadness clutched Gina's heart, swirled through her. "He never told me."

"My guess is he didn't want to burden you with it or pressure you to keep the bike. Ben's not a manipulator, Gina, at least give him that. He's a stand-up guy, even if you think he only considers his own needs. He cares about people—" Cash held her gaze, his voice a mix of frustration and anger "—he cares about you and the kids more than his own life. Getting rid of the bike is one last effort to show you how much he loves you and what he's willing to do for his marriage. Don't let him sell the bike, Gina. Please, don't do it. It will fill him with a regret you can't imagine."

She tried to process what Cash was saying, but it was a struggle. "Why didn't he ever tell me?"

"I told you why. Ben didn't want this to get in the way of your relationship. But if he ditches this bike, regret is going to own him. You've got to stop this." Cash's next words burrowed to her soul. "If you still love him and want this marriage, then damn it, tell him." His voice dipped, turned soft, fierce. "And if you don't, then cut him loose because you're going to end up destroying him."

18

Gina thought about Cash's words for the rest of the afternoon, and once she'd fed the kids dinner and washed dishes, she called Ben. "We need to talk. Can you come by the house?"

"Uh...sure. I'll be there soon." He arrived twenty minutes later, his expression a mix of curiosity and caution. "Need help with the kids?"

No parent turns down an offer of help, especially when baths are involved. She nodded, pointed to their son, who held out a toy airplane for his father to see. "I'll take Ava." She glanced at Alex, said in a firm voice, "You can show Dad the airplane after your bath." When he opened his mouth and let out a noise that sounded a lot like a protest, she said, "Should I put it away? Or maybe return it to Aunt Tess and Uncle Cash?" The single head shake said no, but the double head shake said he understood.

"Listen to your mother," Ben said. "She always knows best." He glanced at her and his lips pulled into a slow smile. "Duty calls."

The next forty minutes were filled with baths, snacks, bedtime stories, goodnights, and I-love-yous. Gina left Ben in Alex's room with the new airplane and headed downstairs where she poured two glasses of wine and waited for him to finish his goodnights. She had a lot of questions, and they started with the real reason Ben was so attached to his motorcycle.

"Hey."

Gina turned and watched Ben move toward her, his long, lean stride nothing like the unsteady gait he'd had earlier this year. What a difference a little time could make. She motioned for him to sit on the couch next to her, handed him his wine. "I think it's time to talk."

"Okay." Those blue eyes studied her as he eased onto the couch, sipped his wine.

Gina worked up a smile, no small effort considering she hadn't been this close to her husband since the night at the Heart Sent. "Thanks for coming." Pause. "And thanks for helping with the kids."

"Sure."

She set her wine glass on the end table and folded her hands in her lap. "I heard you're selling your motorcycle." Surprise flashed across his face seconds before he buried it with a frown.

"Let me guess. Cash talked to you."

Was that anger or annoyance in his voice? "He did. Why do you want to sell it?"

He shrugged, said in a quiet voice, "It seemed like the logical thing to do."

"Really?" *Tell me about Vince.* "Why?"

Ben cleared his throat, ran a hand through his hair. "It's not like I was going to ride it again, and let's be honest, it's a boulder standing in the way of whatever's keeping us apart." He sighed, cleared his throat again. "Okay, it's not the reason for what's keeping us apart, but it sure as hell is one of the reasons. Call it a good faith effort. I'm selling it as a good faith effort to show I'll do whatever's necessary to make this marriage work."

Sadness clouded those blue eyes. And was that desperation on his face? A bleakness that said empty and alone? Had *she* done this to him? "It wasn't right for me to expect you to get rid of the bike."

Another shrug. "You never flat-out asked me, but if this gives us a chance to start over, I'm willing to do it."

"Ben—"

"Does it give us a chance, Gina?"

Cash's words burst through her. *Don't let him sell the bike, Gina. Please, don't do it. It will fill him with a regret you can't imagine.* She opened her mouth, let the truth fall out. "You can't sell the bike, Ben."

His dark brows pinched together, his lips pulled into a frown. "It's too late, isn't it?" His voice turned hoarse, cracked, split open. "No more chances." He leaned back against the couch, closed his eyes.

"Ben." She inched forward, placed a hand on his arm.

"Just give me a minute."

Gina studied her husband, took in the strong jaw, the full lips, the long lashes. Such a handsome man. Who wouldn't want him? Want to be with him? But it was about more than his looks. Ben was a good person, a man who believed in family and commitment, and while he'd gotten sidetracked with the insecurities from the accident, she should have known he'd never betray her. In her heart, she should have trusted him, should have known he would remain loyal and true because that was real love. But she'd been so unsettled by Emma Hale that she'd questioned everything: Ben's love, his fidelity, his desire to be with her.

When he realized how much he'd hurt her and tried to apologize and make amends, Gina had turned him away. Worse, she'd pushed him out of the house with a legal separation. *A legal separation for heaven's sake!* She'd refused the flowers, the perennial garden bed, the attempts to let her know she was special. All she'd wanted was to make him suffer, to know her pain, and she'd been relentless with her comments about not trusting him, not knowing if she'd ever trust him again.

And then what had she done?

Gina blinked back tears as she recalled the night at the Heart Sent and the follow-up talk where she'd suggested no-strings sex instead of getting back together. Of course, he'd refused, because Ben Reed was a decent human being who did the right thing and cared about her—all of her—not just the part he shared in bed. He wanted to be her husband, have a chance to show her how much he loved her and hoped to be part of their family again, but she'd turned him down.

Made him wait and made him suffer.

Forced him to remember over and over how he'd been distant and turned her away.

Listened to Emma Hale and refused Gina's help.

Now he wanted to sell his bike because he believed he had nothing left to give.

This would be the ultimate sacrifice.

She could not let him do it.

Because she loved him, loved him with her whole heart.

She was the one who should ask *him* for a second chance.

Gina leaned toward him, stroked his jaw. "Tell me about Vince."

He inched his eyes open, studied her for several seconds before he spoke. "He was my riding buddy. We met in the police academy and started talking bikes. Next thing we know, we're heading to West Virginia. Beautiful riding there. Mountains, and the clearest skies. Vince wanted to move there." His voice drifted, filled with remembering. "He said he was going to build a log cabin and live off the land and be the best damn policeman West Virginia ever saw." Pause, followed by a long sigh. "Three weeks after we graduated, he was diagnosed with bone cancer. They amputated his left leg below the knee. Vince was still determined to get to West Virginia, but..."

Gina clasped his arm, held tight. "I'm so sorry."

"After he passed, I vowed to ride in his memory. I had the gas tank on my bike painted with Vince's badge and number and the words *Always in the rearview* to remind me how I used to see him in my rearview mirror on our trips." He pinched the bridge of his nose, cleared his throat. "Vince was a good guy who died too soon." Ben dragged his gaze to hers, blinked. "That's why I never wanted to get rid of the bike."

"But why didn't you tell me?"

He shrugged. "I knew how you felt about motorcycles, and I didn't want to lay that guilt on you."

"Oh, Ben..." She trailed a finger along his jaw. "I wish I'd known."

"I was trying to spare you." His blue eyes turned dark. "I wasn't trying to keep it from you, I swear I wasn't."

"I believe you," she whispered.

"I meant what I said before; I'll sell it if that gives us another chance."

"No. I won't ask you to do that." Gina reached for his hand, laced her fingers through his. "I can't say I want you to ride it just yet, but I don't want you to get rid of it."

He held her gaze, said in a voice filled with uncertainty and hope, "I've screwed up too much these past months to take anything for granted. Are you saying you're willing to give us another chance?"

Gina placed a soft kiss on his mouth. "I love you, Ben Reed. You own my heart, and the thought of losing you was too painful. I had to shut down to survive. Please don't ever let anyone or anything come between us again." The tears started, slipped from her cheeks to her chin, onto her blouse. "I don't think I could survive it."

Ben framed her face with his strong hands. "I never doubted you, Gina. I doubted myself, and my ability to be the man you married. The accident messed up my head, made me question my life and what I was doing here. It was a dark time and I'm sorry I dragged you into it."

This might not be the moment to remind her husband that wasn't exactly what happened, but Gina had waited so long to say it and she was getting it out. "I wanted to help you because I knew how tough recovery can be for a man like you, but you shut me out, Ben. That drove us further apart and made you perfect hunting for the person who shall remain nameless." She raised a brow, frowned. "The one whose name shall never be mentioned in this household again."

"If I never hear that name again, I'll be fine with that."

"So, apparently, your cousin Paige is the one we have to thank for the person who shall remain nameless's appearance in Magdalena."

"Paige? What did she have to do with Emma—I mean, that woman?"

"Well, they took a yoga class together and your cousin mentioned this wonderful small town where life was beautiful, and everyone was family."

"How do you know this? Did you hire out Lester Conroy?"

Gina shook her head. "Natalie told me."

"Nate's old—" he caught himself, reworked the comment "—I mean, the cousin you can't stand?"

For most of Gina's life, that statement had been true, but not anymore. "She's not the same person she used to be, and I owe her a lot. She's the one who's responsible for convincing the person who shall remain nameless to leave town."

"No kidding? Maybe I should send her flowers, or a big box of chocolates, or—"

"Why don't you just say hello when you see her, maybe have a chat? That's what she really wants."

"I can do that." He rubbed his jaw, nodded. "Absolutely."

"Speaking of cousins...let's talk about Paige." Gina narrowed her gaze, said in a firm voice, "This is the same cousin who waltzed into town with you and caused problems for Cash and Tess. I'm sure you remember *that* incident?"

He let out a loud sigh. "Yeah, I remember." His blue gaze shifted, slid from her neck to the opening of her blouse. "And I remember you, too. Feisty little thing."

"There is nothing little about me." Pause, a tiny smile. "But thank you."

Ben pulled her close, held her so tight she had to sip air to get a full breath. She didn't care. Not. One. Bit. "It is so good to have my wife back." He released his hold, tilted her chin up with his thumb and forefinger. "I've missed you so damn much."

"I've missed you, too."

"We have a lot of catching up to do." He fingered the opening of her blouse, released the first button.

"Yes, we do." She eased his T-shirt from his jeans, slid a hand over his belly. "I do love the feel of your skin."

"Is that why you wanted the sex without strings?" His lips twitched.

"That was not one of my finer moments. I don't know what I wanted other than to protect myself from getting hurt again. But after that night, I was so confused, I'd try anything."

"Hmm...I like the sound of that." He flipped open three more buttons, pushed the blouse aside to reveal a pink lace bra. "Perfect." He traced the edges of the lace, dipped a finger beneath the fabric. "How about we try the sex *with* strings? I think I like the sound of that." Ben's gaze narrowed on the flesh peeking from the top of her bra. "A lot."

"Me, too." She clasped his hand, stood, and pressed her body against his, letting him know just how much she wanted him. The kiss came next, filled with love, hope, desire, and years of promises. When Gina pulled back, she didn't miss the heat in his gaze or the short choppy breaths that said he wanted her.

"I love you, Gina." He stroked her hair, sifted it between his fingers. "I'll always love you."

A smile of pure joy burst from her. "Let's go to bed. Our bed. The one you belong in."

His lips pulled into a slow smile. "Wherever you are, is where I want to be."

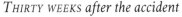

THIRTY WEEKS after the accident

Gina Reed was a no-nonsense, practical kind of woman who didn't need jewelry, clothes, or fancy shows of affection to know her husband cared. How many times had she told him these past weeks that what she wanted couldn't be bought: love, trust, and truth?

He'd given her all of these, and if she stretched the love definition to lovemaking, well, he'd delivered extra on that one. But it wasn't enough, not for Ben, who still woke in the middle of the night just to make sure Gina was sleeping next to him. Good fortune had brought her back to him, and he was going to make sure she stayed. Couldn't a person show gratitude with a pair of diamond earrings? And what about a new watch? He could have gone *really* high-end, but he'd settled for efficient and practical in a pricey brand. Next up were the shoes he'd read about that were made for people who stood a lot and worked on hard-surface floors. Sure, they were expensive, but he'd found a catalog...

"Ben, you have to stop."

"Huh?" *Where had he left the catalog? Was it in the bathroom? The living room?*

"Ben! Did you hear me?" Gina handed him a beer, slid into the kitchen chair next to him.

"I'm sorry, babe, what did you say?" A scowl crept over her lips, followed by a narrowed gaze. Not good. Ben reached for her hand, brought it to his lips and kissed each finger. That usually distracted her enough to lose the scowl.

Her voice gentled and the scowl relaxed. "You've got to stop buying me gifts. It's not necessary."

"I know, but I want to..." He kissed the palm of her hand. "I like to give you things." Another kiss, a dart of his tongue...

Gina squirmed, pulled her hand away, and cleared her throat. "I'm not talking about *that*."

For a woman who'd suggested no-strings sex and let him enjoy every part of her body, she still blushed when he referred to sex. Ben smiled, let his voice dip in what his wife called sexy-seductive. "I'm glad you're satisfied." Another smile. "You *are* satisfied, aren't you?" He rubbed his jaw, let out a quiet sigh. "I only heard one *more* last night and not a single *don't stop*. Should I be worried?"

She swatted his arm, the blush creeping from the swell of her breasts to her neck, splashing her cheeks. "You are no gentleman."

He laughed, patted his knee, and said, "Come here. Let me show you why you don't want me to be a gentleman." Her lips twitched and her eyes sparkled seconds before she scooted off the chair and onto his right knee. His good knee. Some days he almost forgot about the accident, but then there were the reminders, some physical, some not, that said it had been real and life-changing.

"You are one crazy husband, do you know that?" She ran her fingers through his hair, played with the curls.

"Crazy in love? Yeah, that's me." He stroked her back, considered the lead-in for the next subject. "So, I'm going to slow down on the gifts."

"Good, because you can't buy what I want." Her voice turned serious, her dark eyes bright. "I want you, Ben, all of you." Pause, a sniff. "Even the part that gets scared and unsure. That part I want most of all, so I can be there for you, with you...so we can get through it together."

He nodded, cleared his throat, and managed, "Thank you."

She placed a soft kiss on his mouth, murmured, "What's the gift and it better not cost more than a dollar."

"How'd you know I wanted to get you another gift?"

Gina pulled back, studied him. "*Is* this about another gift?"

"One more. Maybe two." Her sigh said she thought he was being overboard ridiculous. Well, she hadn't heard about these shoes. "I found a catalog with special shoes in it that are supposed to be great for people who stand all day and work on hard surfaces. They have some extra support and arch stuff in them. I thought you could take a look? Maybe order a pair?" Her expression softened and damn, was that a tear slipping down her cheek? "Gina? You don't like that idea?"

She swiped at her cheek, smiled. "Yes, Ben, I do like that idea. It's so kind and thoughtful." Pause, a swallow, and then a whispered "So filled with love."

Ah, so the shoes were a go. Gina's yes made him bold and he pushed his next idea. "Just one more thing. What about a composting bin?"

"What do you know about composting bins?"

The look she gave him was part curious, part admiration. "What do you think I was doing all those nights at the Heart Sent?" It was his turn to fight the heat creeping up his neck. "It made me feel close to you, and the more I read about it, the more I got hooked. Do you know there are green and brown ingredients and indoor composters and compost tea? I figured if we got another chance, maybe we could make this a family project." He shrugged, looked away. "If you think you might want to do it. I know it's late in the season, but..."

Gina threw her hands around his neck, hugged him, and let out a laugh that sounded a lot like pure delight. When she pulled back, she stroked his jaw, her eyes filled with tears. "I love the idea, Ben. Love it. Forget the jewelry and the blingy stuff." A soft kiss on the mouth, then another. "Get ready for the tears."

He smiled. "Good tears?"

She sniffed. "Oh, yes, definitely good tears."

"Gina?" He swiped the first tear with the pad of his thumb. "There's one more gift."

"Ben—"

"You'll like this one, too. It's not jewelry. I call it a gift for our family. You'll see it tonight." Ben refused to say more despite Gina's questions and guesses.

A new car? Please tell me you did not buy a new car.

Nope.

Tickets to Renova's flower festival?

No tickets.

Lots of sighs. *A jungle gym, kind of like the one in Harry Blacksworth's backyard?*

Uh...no.

A scowl...two scowls... *Did you get us a puppy?*

A puppy? He hadn't considered that. But... *Do you want a puppy? I think I like that idea.*

No puppy. Her voice dipped, softened. *When Ava turns two, we can talk about a dog...not a puppy.*

He'd hid a grin. *Sure.*

The guessing continued through dinner, and once Gina realized she really had no clue what the gift could be, she offered outrageous suggestions: an African safari, a

Caribbean cruise, a tour through Europe, making Ben laugh at her imagination.

"Okay, it's time." Ben peeked through the closed blinds on the sliding glass door leading to the deck. "When I call you, come outside with the kids."

Gina stared at him. "It's a jungle gym like Harry's, isn't it? I told you the kids—"

"Hey—" Ben placed his hands on her shoulders, held her gaze "—it's not a jungle gym." He smiled, kissed her. "It's so much better."

She sighed. "You know I don't like surprises. They make me nervous."

One more kiss before he pulled away and grinned. "Not this one. Give me a few minutes and I'll call you." He disappeared out the back door, checked the extension cords, and hit the switch. *Perfect.* Ben flipped off the switch, inched open the sliding door. "It's time." Seconds later, his wife and kids stood on the deck, staring into the darkness.

"Mom said you wanted to show us something." Alex stood next to Ben, patted his arm. "I don't see anything but stars."

Ben ruffled his son's hair. "Keep looking. Stand right here, and watch." He flipped the switch and the twenty-foot evergreen in the backyard burst into color with Christmas lights. Alex let out a whoop, Ava squealed. Gina gasped, sputtered, "What...when...how?"

Ben scooped Ava from his wife's arms, pulled Gina close. "Call it a lot of careful planning and help from friends. Nate and Cash know how to keep secrets, and they're pretty good at stringing lights."

"That's a tall tree."

No hiding the worry in her voice. "I didn't climb any

ladders," he said, his voice soft, reassuring. "Nate brought one over, and Cash did the climbing."

A sigh. "I'm sure Tess won't like that."

He leaned down, kissed his wife's temple. "He took his time, wore the right shoes, asked for help when he needed it." Like Ben should have done when he'd crawled up the ladder. It was the rushing that did him in. "So, what do you think?"

"It's beautiful."

Ben pulled his wife closer. "I agree."

"Dad, what's that light over there?" Alex pointed to the narrow path of light zeroing in on the other side of the tree.

"Hmm, why don't we go see?"

Alex tore down the steps and raced toward the light. "It's Mr. Snowman!"

Ben and Gina followed their son to the other side of the evergreen and the newest addition to the Reed Christmas decorations: Mr. Snowman. "I figured we needed a new Mr. Snowman since I sort of destroyed the old one."

Alex squinted at the plastic snowman. "This one's shinier. I'm glad he's ours, aren't you, Mom?"

"Yes, I'm very glad he's ours."

Ben glanced at his wife, but she wasn't looking at Mr. Snowman. No indeed, she was looking at Ben. He smiled, kissed her. "We didn't get to celebrate Christmas together." His voice dipped, filled with love for the woman next to him. "So, I figured we could celebrate it now." The smile his wife gave him said she liked that idea. A lot.

"But Dad? Where're the gifts?"

Ben eased a hand on his son's shoulder, pulled him close. "The gifts are right here, son. You, Ava, Mom, and me. We call it family and there's no better gift than that."

EPILOGUE

Pop settled back in his chair, looked up at the portrait of his wife, and smiled. "Oh, Lucy, but you would be proud of this town and the way they pitched in to help Ben and Gina Reed. You always talked about team effort and said when it came time to pass the torch, a body had to be ready and prepared. I'm not saying I'm ready for that just yet, but it's a good idea to get the town ready for when the time comes."

He eased a pizzelle off the plate, nibbled. Nothing like one of these with his morning coffee. Lily had convinced him to come to Barbara's Boutique and Bakery this afternoon to help mix up a batch. He still wasn't keen on the idea of seeing them sold, said pizzelles should be given as a gift. But Lily and his granddaughter, Lucy, had teamed up and given him a slew of reasons pizzelles should be sold in the bakery. It was the last that struck him the hardest and made him change his mind: *You can't keep up with the pizzelle baking and everyone in Magdalena should be able to get one*. He'd only agreed if they promised to sell the pizzelles cheap. Period.

Those two were always in cahoots over one thing or another, figuring out new plans and marketing schemes, making flyers, contacting Tony for ideas on advertising. The boy had a nose for the stuff, and since "selling a story" had been his line of work for a lot of years, Pop figured that made him an expert. Tony said the name had to go, even suggested a few replacements, but Lucy shook her head, and vowed there'd be no name change without the previous owner's approval. Good luck with that one.

Pop pushed aside the pizzelle drama and thought about the goings-on these past several months and his less-than-hands-on contribution. Didn't mean he wasn't involved, because he was, but this time was different. "I have to admit it wasn't easy to sit back and watch all the goings-on between the Reeds and not step in." He chuckled, shook his head. "But you know me, I still had my hand in the mix. Mimi called me the second Natalie Servetti Trimble left the Heart Sent all worried about an interloper trying to destroy Ben and Gina Reed. I even had a few conversations with Lester Conroy and had him check out Emma Hale before anybody else did. I got to hand it to Natalie; I never thought I'd say this, but she's shaping into a nice girl. Now, I know what you're thinking about that comment, but I've seen it and I've heard it. She and Gina are even talking again, and there was some mention about inviting the kids to a birthday party. Not sure what that's about, but I'll find out."

The trip to California and the cataract operations had taken Pop out of Magdalena for a bit and when he returned, Ben and Gina Reed were knee-deep in trouble, and not just because Ben had a busted knee. Harry had kept him informed but hearing it after the fact was a lot different than direct observation and conversations at Lina's Café. That's how a person gathered real information. Pop had to hand it to Ben's buddies, Nate and Cash, for getting their friend to see common sense and not ditching him when he played the fool. Most men did play the fool a time or two in their life, and an injured man close to forty was prime picking.

Pop rubbed his jaw, remembered when he'd been thirty-nine and had a few shenanigans in the fool category. He'd outgrown them, and Ben had, too. No doubt, the boy loved his wife, loved being married, and he sure did love those kids. "I talked to Gina the other day, that woman glows. I mean one-hundred-watt glows, and I know it has to do with her husband. Still can't get over how he brought Christmas to their backyard. It's been four weeks now and every night that tree lights up and the Mr. Snowman, too. People talk about it, some laugh and call them crazy, but most smile and say they'd like to see an expression of love like that, too. Indeed, wouldn't we all? And I think I heard talk of a dog. Can't be sure, but I think so." *Goodness, a dog to go with two little ones?*

"Speaking of dogs, Harry's got it bad. You'd think that rescue was a prince." He chuckled, thought of Harry's dog. "Guess I'm no better. Do you know I let Cooper in the house, even let him drink out of my cereal bowl? The dog loves pizzelles. I know, I know... I shouldn't be feeding him people food, but I only give him the scraps when I trim the pizzelles." He chuckled again, pictured the dog gobbling up those tiny scraps like it was filet mignon. "He's a keeper. Harry says they're both rescues and that's why they under-stand each other." Pop smiled at that. "I have to say, I agree."

"There's been rumblings about somebody coming back to town, but I call baloney on that. What that family did to that boy all those years ago is unforgiveable, but at least he got away. There's no way he'd come back. My gut tells me the rumblings are hopes with no air in them, like a cream puff that didn't rise. But just in case, I'll keep my ears peeled, and listen... People will bring me the details and I'll cobble them together. Maybe I'll involve Harry, see if he's honed his skills because one of these days I'm pretty sure he'll be the one to take my place. What do you think, Lucy? Do you think Harry Blacksworth's got what it takes to help this town in and out of its misery? Show them about forgiveness and redemption?" Pop leaned back, closed his eyes, and thought on that. "Yup, I think he might be the one. He just needs a little practice and I'll see he gets it."

~

I HOPE you enjoyed *A Family Affair: The Choice* and "meeting" Cooper. My editor wrote and told me she was glad to learn how Cooper got his name... Well, that part of Cooper's story was pure fiction because he came to us already named. When I wrote this scene, I envisioned Harry Blacksworth looking down that snowy road as an animal approached and imagining Gary Cooper in High Noon. It just seems like something Harry would do, doesn't it?

As ALWAYS, many thanks for choosing to spend your time reading *A Family Affair: The Choice*. Please consider writing a review on the site where you purchased it.

Want to find out about new releases, sneak peeks, and what's happening in my world? Sign up at http://www.marycampisi.com

NEXT UP IS *A Family Affair: The Proposal* but it's not the kind of proposal you think!

ABOUT THE AUTHOR

Mary Campisi writes emotion-packed books about second chances. Whether contemporary romances, women's fiction, or Regency historicals, her books all center on belief in the beauty of that second chance. Her small town romances center around family life, friendship, and forgiveness as they explore the issues of today's contemporary women.

Mary should have known she'd become a writer when at age thirteen she began changing the ending to all the books she read. It took several years and a number of jobs, including registered nurse, receptionist in a swanky hair salon, accounts payable clerk, and practice manager in an OB/GYN office, for her to rediscover writing. Enter a mouse-less computer, a floppy disk, and a dream large enough to fill a zip drive. The rest of the story lives on in every book she writes.

When she's not working on her craft or following the lives of five adult children, Mary's digging in the dirt with her flowers and herbs, cooking, reading, walking her rescue lab mix, Cooper, or, on the perfect day, riding off into the sunset with her very own hero/husband on his Harley Ultra Limited.

If you would like to be notified when Mary has a new release, please sign up at:

http://www.marycampisi.com/newsletter.

To learn more about Mary and her books...
https://www.marycampisi.com
mary@marycampisi.com

:fb: facebook.com/marycampisibooks

:twitter: twitter.com/MaryCampisi

:instagram: instagram.com/marycampisiauthor

:amazon: amazon.com/author/marycampisi

:bookbub: bookbub.com/authors/mary-campisi

OTHER BOOKS BY MARY CAMPISI

Contemporary Romance:

Truth in Lies Series
Book One: *A Family Affair*
Book Two: *A Family Affair: Spring*
Book Three: *A Family Affair: Summer*
Book Four: *A Family Affair: Fall*
Book Five: *A Family Affair: Christmas*
Book Six: *A Family Affair: Winter*
Book Seven: *A Family Affair: The Promise*
Book Eight: *A Family Affair: The Secret*
Book Nine: *A Family Affair: The Wish*
Book Ten: *A Family Affair: The Gift*
Book Eleven: *A Family Affair: The Weddings, a novella*
Book Twelve: *A Family Affair: The Cabin, a novella*
Book Thirteen: *A Family Affair: The Return*
Book Fourteen: *A Family Affair: The Choice*
Book Fifteen: *A Family Affair: The Proposal*
A Family Affair Boxed Set: Books 1-3
A Family Affair Boxed Set 2: Books 4-6
Meals From Magdalena: A Family Affair Cookbook

NEW: Park Bench series:

Book One: *A Family Affair Shorts: Destiny*

Book Two: *A Family Affair Shorts: Regret*

Book Three: *A Family Affair Shorts: Love*

Book Four: *A Family Affair Shorts: Heartbreak*

Book Five: *A Family Affair Shorts: Peace*

A Family Affair Shorts Boxed Set

NEW: Reunion Gap Series

Book Zero: *Christmas in Reunion Gap*, a novelette

Book One: *Strangers Like Us*

Book Two: *Liars Like Us*

Book Three: *Lovers Like Us*

More to come…

That Second Chance Series

Book One: *Pulling Home*

Book Two: *The Way They Were*

Book Three: *Simple Riches*

Book Four: *Paradise Found*

Book Five: *Not Your Everyday Housewife*

Book Six: *The Butterfly Garden*

That Second Chance Boxed Set 1-3

That Second Chance Boxed Set 4-6

That Second Chance Complete Boxed Set 1-6

The Betrayed Trilogy

Book One: *Pieces of You*

Book Two: *Secrets of You*

Book Three: *What's Left of Her*: a novella

The Betrayed Trilogy Boxed Set

Regency Historical:

An Unlikely Husband Series

Book One - *The Seduction of Sophie Seacrest*

Book Two - *A Taste of Seduction*

Book Three - *A Touch of Seduction*, a novella

Book Four - *A Scent of Seduction*

An Unlikely Husband Boxed Set

The Model Wife Series

Book One: *The Redemption of Madeline Munrove*

Young Adult:

Pretending Normal

Made in the USA
Lexington, KY
30 July 2019